DAWN AND WHITNEY, FRIENDS FOR EVER

Ann M. Martin

Hippo

The author gratefully acknowledges
Nola Thacker
for her help in

Scholastic Children's Books,
Commonwealth House, 1–19 New Oxford Street,
London WC1A 1NU, UK
a division of Scholastic Ltd
London ~ New York ~ Toronto ~ Sydney ~ Auckland

First published in the US by Scholastic Inc., 1994
First published in the UK by Scholastic Ltd, 1996

ISBN 0 590 13795 6

Typeset by Rowland Phototypesetting Ltd, Bury St Edmunds,
Suffolk
Printed by Cox & Wyman Ltd, Reading, Berks.

10 9 8 7 6 5 4 3 2 1

1st CHAPTER

Sunny, sunny California.

That's tautology. If you don't know that word, it means that you don't need to say that the sun is always shining in California. Just the word California says it all.

Do I sound as if I like living here? I do. Maybe it's no coincidence, either, that my father's nickname for me is Sunshine. Or that one of my two best friends in California is called Sunny.

And summer in California is California to the full. Surf's up. Minimum clothing needed. Sunscreen and shades and . . . well, you get the idea.

Dawn Schafer (that's me) of Stoneybrook, Connecticut and Palo City, California, was about to settle in for a *smooth* summer in the sunny California sun. (Oh,

OK, California isn't *always* sunny and warm, but it feels that way to me.)

I suppose I do sound rather like a tourist, the ones you see on the beaches sometimes with cameras and big flowery shirts and weird sunglasses, snapping pictures of everything that moves. But I was actually born and brought up in California. I never really appreciated it, though, till my mother and father got divorced and my mum moved back to her home town, Stoneybrook, Connecticut, with me and my younger brother, Jeff. That's where her parents, our grandparents, Granny and Pop-Pop, still live.

Naturally I wasn't too enthusiastic about the move. But we bought this old farmhouse built in the 1700s and I actually discovered a secret passageway from my bedroom to the barn. Then I made friends with Mary Anne Spier and she invited me to join a group called the Baby-sitters Club (or the BSC) and soon I was pretty happy.

Not my brother Jeff, though. He went from obnoxious-but-lovable little brother to monster brother and he even started getting into trouble at school. He wanted to go back to California, and eventually Mum and Dad decided that might be best.

I hated to see Jeff go. In such a short time we'd gone from being a family of four in one place, to a bi-coastal divorced family, two here, two there.

But not for long. Mary Anne's father and my mother rediscovered each other. They'd known each other at high school and gone out together and then lost touch. But the romance rekindled and they got married. (Mary Anne's mother had died when she was just a baby and she and her father had been a family of two for practically her whole life.) So anyway, Mary Anne and her father moved into the farmhouse together with Mary Anne's grey tabby kitten Tigger. As Mary Anne and I were already best friends, things couldn't get any better than that, right?

Wrong.

I kept on missing Dad and Jeff. And the harder I tried not to miss them, the worse it got. Not California. I mean, I missed it, but I could live without it. My father and my brother were a different story, though. At last I decided I had to go west again for more than a visit.

It was a difficult decision. It made Mary Anne cry (which made me cry, too), and it made Mum pretty miserable, especially as she took it personally. But eventually

3

she and Dad worked it out (along with the guidance counsellors at Stoneybrook Middle School and at Vista, my California school, who had to make sure I would have "continuity of education" if I moved back to California for any length of time). And I came back to Palo City for a good, long stay.

The right decision. A hard decision, but the right one. I'll be going back to Stoneybrook before too much longer but, right now, I'm enjoying every minute of the west coast part of my bi-coastal life.

Well, almost every minute.

It's this dating thing, you see.

I mean, there are plenty of nice people out here, but. . .

Oh, I'm not talking about *me*! I mean our father. You see, he's been dating a lot recently. Especially since he broke off his engagement to Carol, this woman he'd been seeing for a long time. I admit, I was relieved when they broke up. Not that I didn't like Carol. But she tried *so* hard to be cool that it left me cold. I realize now that I didn't understand how hard it must have been for Carol, too, coming into a ready-made family and trying to fit in. About a hundred times worse than being the new kid in school!

But anyway, that's over and Dad is

doing what Granny calls "playing the field". That means he's dating a lot. And a lot of different kinds of people.

It also means that after the first couple of dates, the "date me, date my kids" part goes into action. That means that on the next date, Dad includes Jeff and me.

Try to imagine going on a date—which includes your parents. Pretty weird, isn't it?

Well, it must be pretty weird for dad and his dates, too. I'm glad he wants us to like the people he goes out with. But I keep thinking there must be an easier way. . .

"What's for dinner?" Jeff zoomed through the kitchen on his way to his next rendezvous with chaos, and I grabbed hold of him.

"Endive salad, three-cheese macaroni, asparagus and fruit pie," I said. "And you're in charge of laying the table."

"Endive?" Jeff clutched his throat and Mrs Bruen, our housekeeper, laughed.

"You've never had endive, Jeff," Mrs Bruen said. It was true. Jeff just liked giving me aggro little-brother style.

Jeff let go of his throat and I let go of his jeans and a cunning look came into his eyes. "Hey," he said.

5

I recognized the look, a hangover from his most recent career plan to become a comedian, which meant that he told a zillion bad jokes to anybody who was unwary enough to stand still for one second.

I groaned, but Jeff went on. "Hey, Dawn, Mrs Bruen, what did the dog—"

Just then the doorbell rang.

"Has Dad got a date?" Jeff asked.

"Yes," I said. "But it's too early. That must be Sunny. She's staying the night."

I wiped my hands on a kitchen towel, put the fruit pie in a safe place on the worktop, ready to pop into the oven when we sat down for dinner, and went to open the door.

"Dawn!" cried Sunny, as if we hadn't talked on the phone only a couple of hours before.

I've known Sunshine Daydream Winslow longer than I've known anybody else in my whole life (except my mother and father and my grandparents, of course). Her parents, as you might guess from Sunny's name, were (and still are, I suppose) hippies. The Winslows live down the road from us and Mrs Winslow is a potter, an artist and a really nice human being. Come to think of it, she's a lot like another artist I know, a fellow member of the BSC back in Stoneybrook, Claudia Kishi. But more about that later.

"Sunny!" I exclaimed now, matching her tone and grinning. Sunny bounded in, slung her rucksack into the nearest corner and sniffed appreciatively. "What's cooking? It smells like one of my favourite foods."

"Three-cheese macaroni." It's a Mrs Bruen speciality and it *is* one of Sunny's favourites.

"Great!" exclaimed Sunny.

"Yes, I like it too," I told her.

Sunny and I are a lot alike. Not only is her name the same as my nickname, but we're both blonde, although Sunny is a strawberry blonde and my hair is almost white. We also like natural food and don't eat red meat, and we're independent, outgoing and easy-going. We like surfing. We *love* ghost stories.

"I'm starving," said Sunny as we went into the kitchen.

"You're just in time. Jeff's laying the table now." I raised my voice so that Jeff, who I could see edging out of the kitchen, could hear me.

Jeff stopped. Then he went over to the cutlery drawer, scooped up a handful of knives, forks and spoons and headed for the dining room.

"Hey, Jeff-man," said Sunny. "How's it going?"

Jeff stopped. That cunning look came into his eyes. "Hey, Sunny! Listen. What did the dog—"

"Table first, jokes second," I intervened quickly. "And you know what, Jeff? You should wait till Dad gets here. Then he can hear your joke, too."

"OK," said Jeff. He took one of the dinner knives, stuck it under his arm, cried, "I've been *stabbed*!" and reeled away.

Mrs Bruen rolled her eyes.

"Anything I can do to help?" asked Sunny.

"It's all done," said Mrs Bruen, opening the oven and pulling out the casserole.

Jeff came back in, grabbed the plates, and rushed out. This time he didn't waste any time. Everything smelled too good.

It *was* good, too. Our father came in and sat at the table with us (although he couldn't eat; he was going to take his latest date to dinner after a film). Jeff got to tell his joke. And Sunny and I laughed a lot and settled down to concentrate on macaroni and asparagus.

"What film are you going to see, Mr Schafer?" Sunny asked.

"We're going to a Charlie Chaplin film festival," my father said.

"That sounds cool," said Sunny.

"Could be," said my father. He winked at me and I tried to smile encouragingly.

"You'll have a good time," I said. Then I thought, good grief! I sound just like someone's parents. The next thing I know, I'll be telling Dad just to be himself.

Dad added to the feeling by saying as he stood up to go, "Do I look OK?"

"Super," said Sunny, and I nodded.

"See you later, then," my father said.

"We'll save you some dessert," answered Jeff. "Ha, ha!"

When dinner was over (and Jeff had, despite his best efforts, not eaten all the fruit pie), and Mrs Bruen had left, Sunny and I were the babysitters in charge, informally.

We followed Jeff out into the garden. Half a dozen kids were out in their own gardens around us, or zooming up and down the pavements on roller blades and bicycles. But when Jeff said, "football," it wasn't long before we had a game of football organized with the other kids, with Sunny and me playing goalie at either end. It was fun, kind of like the Krushers' softball games back in Stoneybrook. (The Krushers are a softball team made up of kids of all ages—the average age is 5.8.) Everyone played hard but fair and when Jeff scored a goal against me and shouted, "Goal, Schafer!" everyone cheered good-naturedly along with him.

When it got too dark for that, we went back indoors and settled down to watch a film. Not much later, I noticed that Jeff's eyes were closing. Sunny and I exchanged glances. We knew better than to suggest that Jeff might be getting sleepy. He's ten and rather touchy about being treated "like a baby".

"I'm getting tired," I said to Sunny, but looking at Jeff.

She knew exactly what I meant. She stretched and yawned and said, "Me, too."

Jeff opened his eyes, squinted at the screen for a moment, then said, "Me, too. See you!"

"I'll come and say goodnight in a little while," I said.

"OK," said Jeff.

"Brush your teeth," I called after him.

"OK."

"So how sleepy *are* you?" asked Sunny.

"Not at all," I said. "Besides, it's not *that* late." How late was it in Connecticut? I wondered.

Sunny, my oldest-friend-and-mind-reader, asked, "How late is it in Connecticut? Not too late for a phone call, right?"

I flashed her a grin. "Right!"

A few minutes later (three hours later in Connecticut), I heard Mary Anne's voice on the phone.

"Dawn! It's you! Where are you?"

"California still," I said.

Mary Anne laughed. "And we still miss you in Stoneybrook. What's happening?" We talked for a while. I updated her on my father's new dating plan and what was happening in the We ♥ Kids Club (which is the more laid-back California version of the Babysitters Club back in Stoneybrook), and she told me what was happening with the BSC. We didn't talk too long—after all, if my father had a huge phone bill, he might object to my phoning Connecticut so much—but it was long enough to be satisfying.

Afterwards, I went to say goodnight to Jeff, which turned out to be unnecessary, and by the time I got back to help Sunny make popcorn, Dad was coming home from his date.

"How was it?" I said as he walked into the kitchen.

"The popcorn was good," said Dad.

"And?" asked Sunny.

"I liked the film. *The Gold Rush*. It's one of my favourite Chaplin films."

"And?" I prompted.

"That's it," said my dad.

"You have to kiss a lot of frogs before you can find a prince. Or a princess," said Sunny.

"What?" I shrieked. I've known Sunny for ever. But I've never heard her say that.

Sunny went bright red.

My father burst out laughing. "Thanks for the advice, Sunny. And I know you're right. Some day my frog princess will come."

My father was still laughing as he went into his room.

And I was still teasing Sunny about what she'd said when we went to sleep late that night, after talking through one and a half scary videos and eating another bowl of popcorn.

2nd CHAPTER

"This meeting of the We Love Kids Club will now come to order," I intoned.

Silence.

I looked around the room.

Sunny's mouth dropped open.

Maggie Blume gave a theatrical little gasp.

Jill Henderson looked at me with real concern in her chocolate brown eyes and said, "Dawn? Are you feeling OK?"

I couldn't help it. I burst out laughing. After a moment, Sunny and Maggie started laughing, too, and Jill grinned sheepishly.

The reason they were laughing was because that was definitely *not* the way we run our club. Sunny started the W♥KC when I was in Stoneybrook, after I'd told her about the Babysitters Club I'd joined there.

The BSC is still going strong in Stoneybrook and I'm still a member. (Basically.) And every Monday, Wednesday and Friday afternoon from five-thirty to six (Stoneybrook time) I can tell you exactly what my closest friends and fellow BSC members are doing. They're sitting in Claudia Kishi's room having a BSC meeting. Kristy Thomas is the chairman and one of the founder members of the BSC. She got the idea one night while listening to her mother make a zillion phone calls trying to find a babysitter for her little brother. What (Kristy the ideas queen thought) what if a person could make just one phone call and reach several babysitters at once?

Now, at exactly five-thirty Stoneybrook time, Kristy is sitting in her director's chair with her green visor on, saying, "This meeting of the BSC will now come to order." Claudia, the vice-chairman, is handing round the junk food that she keeps hidden in strategic places in her room. Mary Anne, who is BSC secretary, is keeping the record book. Stacey McGill, the treasurer, is collecting and counting subs (if it's Monday, subs day). Shannon, who is alternate officer (and my replacement), and responsible for taking over someone else's job in case of emergency, is there. And Jessica Ramsey and Mallory Pike, who are junior officers (they can't babysit at night because they're too young), are there too, talking and laughing and taking care of business.

Which is not exactly the way the We ♥ Kids Club works, as you might have guessed.

We're more laid back. Easy-going.

But not *too* easy-going. That almost got us into trouble not long ago. Our club got written up in the newspaper and then we were featured on a local news station on TV and the next thing we knew, we were swamped with calls. Our, er, loose organizational style meant that we ended up double-booking and overbooking and almost making a real mess out of our business. That's when we decided that laid back didn't mean no rules at all. So we made up a few.

1. Regular meeting times. Every week. At Sunny's.

2. Keep a record book.

Are you waiting for more rules? That's it. No officers. No other special rules. Unless, of course, we decide we need them.

I looked around the room at my fellow

club members, thought about the BSC, and wondered if we'd ever have a BSC/ W♥KC convention.

Hmmm. That would be a job for Kristy Thomas. Kristy is the most organized person in the world, and possibly the universe. She lives with her mother and stepfather, a stepbrother and stepsister (part time), her maternal grandmother, her three brothers (two older, one younger), her adopted little sister, a dog, a cat and a family ghost in a mansion in Stoneybrook. The mansion and the stepfather and stepsiblings came along after her mother recently remarried. Before that, Kristy's mother was working pretty hard as a single parent to bring up four kids. (Kristy's father left when her seven-year-old brother was just a baby and is now rarely in touch).

Kristy has brown hair and brown eyes and is the shortest person in her class. She's a casual dresser, jeans and sweaters mostly, but that's the only thing she's casual about. As I've said before, Kristy is *intensely* organized. She not only thought of the BSC and got it going, but she also thought of the BSC record book, complete with client list and a calendar of each member's sitting jobs (no double-booking or overbooking in the BSC!).

Club members also keep notes and records of their various jobs in the BSC notebook, which all the members use as a sort of reference to keep them up to date with what's happening to the kids they look after.

Mary Anne is Kristy's oldest and best friend, a classic case of opposites attracting, at least personality-wise. Mary Anne and Kristy look rather alike—they're both short and have brown hair and are rather conservative dressers—but Mary Anne is quiet and very shy and sensitive, while Kristy is outspoken and opinionated and occasionally thick-skinned. I've hardly ever seen Kristy cry, but it doesn't take much to bring tears to Mary Anne's eyes. Her boyfriend, Logan, knows he must be prepared when they go to see films that have the least possibility of being sad.

Mary Anne is also my best friend in Stoneybrook and my stepsister, and I think she is a super-excellent friend and sister, *especially* sister. After her mother's death, her father brought her up very strictly (he wanted to be sure he did things properly) and I think that's one of the reasons she's such a terrific sister. She'd never had a brother or sister or a mum before. So when our parents got married and we made up a whole new family, it was a whole new, special thing for Mary Anne in even more ways than it was for me.

Anyway, I miss her patience and the way she listens and how supportive she is, and how stubborn she can be about something she believes in. I know Mary Anne misses me, too, and we try to stay in close touch.

I like to imagine her at the meetings, keeping the record book—and keeping Kristy and the other BSC members in order!

Claudia? Well, she's one of the original members of the BSC and the only member with her own phone line, which is the reason the meetings are at her house in her room. (That and quick access to junk food!) Claud is an artist and one day she's going to be world-famous. But right now she does her art, keeps her look super-cool and uniquely Claudia-esque (she's Japanese-American, with dark eyes and long black hair), and tries not to be bothered by the fact that school work is mostly a mystery to her. Claudia has a genius older sister who thrives on school, but maybe Claudia's beginning to realize, deep down, that she's a genius too, in her own way—an artistic one.

18

Stacey McGill is Claud's best friend and the BSC treasurer. She was born and brought up in New York City, which gives her a distinct "city" style. She moved to Stoneybrook with her parents, moved back to NYC with her parents, then moved to Stoneybrook *again* with her mum when her parents got divorced. Stacey's a maths whizz. She's got long blonde hair (darker than mine), is an only child (like Mary Anne) and, like me, watches what she eats. But Stacey does it because she really has to. She has diabetes, which means her blood sugar level can go haywire. She has to be very careful with her diet and injects herself every day with insulin.

Jessica Ramsey and Mallory Pike are sixth-graders and junior club members, best friends, and talented, too. Jessi is a ballerina who is already taking special classes, while Mallory writes and illustrates her own stories. Both Jessi and Mallory are the oldest in their families. Jessi is the oldest of three kids, and Mal is the oldest of *eight*, which means she came to the BSC with plenty of experience. In fact, her family was, and is, one of the BSC's biggest clients. Mallory has pale white skin with freckles, red hair, glasses and a brace. Jessi has medium brown skin, brown eyes and long legs. Mal and Jessi are crazy about horses.

Logan, Mary Anne's boyfriend, is the other associate member (actually, the only one, now that I'm in California and Shannon is filling in for me). He doesn't attend meetings all that often, but he takes occasional jobs when we can't handle them all. Shannon Kilbourne, who has my job now, used to be an associate member, too. She's Kristy's neighbour and the only BSC member who goes to a private school, Stoneybrook Day School. She's a bit like Kristy—involved in everything, and organized enough to make it look easy.

A babysitters convention. Would it ever happen? And what would it be like?

The phone beeped and we stopped laughing, and Sunny, who was closest to the phone, picked it up. "We Love Kids Club," she said.

And that was how *our* meetings usually came to order.

It was the day after Sunny had slept over at my house and we were at a regular meeting of the We ♥ Kids Club.

I looked around the room at my fellow club members. We are all blonde: I'm the palest, with white blonde hair. Sunny's a strawberry blonde. Maggie's got short golden blonde hair (with purple raccoon streaks over each ear today, to match the long tail of blonde hair braided with purple string hanging down her back). And Jill has dark golden hair.

We're all health food fans, too. But that doesn't mean we don't eat snacks at our meetings, too. Our snacks just tend towards the fruits and nuts and yogurt variety instead of crisps and cakes and sugar-frosted cereal (yes, Claudia's been known to eat sugar-frosted cereal straight out of the packet).

Sunny put her hand over the receiver and announced the job. We all looked at each other, and Maggie said, "I can do it. I think."

Jill pulled out the record book from under a pile of books on Sunny's desk and tossed it across the room to Maggie, who flipped through. She ran her finger down the page.

"Yes, no problem," said Maggie, scrawling her name and the time on the date.

Sunny nodded and got back on the phone to confirm.

See? Much more casual than the BSC.

Maggie swapped the record book for our version of the club notebook—our own personal health-food cookbook. "I know there's a recipe for tofu-vegetable kebabs in here somewhere," she muttered.

"A barbecue?" asked Sunny, suddenly paying attention. (Food is our favourite shared interest).

"Yes." Maggie shrugged. "My dad has some people coming in from Hollywood and he's doing this barbecue thing." She wrinkled up her nose. "I *think* snails are involved." We all shrieked and began making gross suggestions as Maggie flipped through the book.

Maggie wasn't kidding—about the snails or Hollywood. Her father is in the film business and stars go in and out of her house. And she lives in a mansion, too. It's California-style, with a landscaped pool (natural shape, not square), a screening room, a gym and dozens and dozens of rooms. Her kitchen is so big you could rollerblade in it.

But to Maggie, it's no big deal. It's not that she's trying to be super-cool and pretend it doesn't matter. It's just that she's used to it, I suppose.

Maggie keeps her hair short and punkish (as you might have guessed from my description of it) with clothes to match, like a favourite leather bomber jacket that she wears come rain or shine, hot or cold.

She'd brought it with her today, and was wearing it over a black cropped tank-top, leopard-print leggings, and black lace-up boots.

Jill reached over and pointed. "You've just passed the recipe, Mag."

"Oh, right."

Jill smiled. "Snails," she said. "Ugh!" And then, "Poor snails. . ."

She was only half kidding. Jill is probably the most serious of us, and she's sensitive in ways that remind me of Mary Anne sometimes. Jill lives with her mum and older sister Liz in the hills at the edge of town, together with three huge boxer dogs: Spike, Shakespeare and Smee. She's the only one of us who doesn't live in the neighbourhood and she usually takes the bus to meetings. Like the rest of us, Jill likes surfing. And she's really good at it, too.

The phone rang again and Jill picked it up. "We Love Kids Club," she said. The little smile on her face turned into a serious expression as she listened. "Oh," she said. "Mmm. Well, we need to check our schedule book. We'll call you right back."

We all looked at Jill in surprise as she wrote down the caller's name and phone number and rang off.

"Wow!" said Sunny. "What was *that* all about?"

"A new client. Mr Cater," Jill said.

"New clients are good," said Maggie encouragingly. "What is it? A problem child? We can handle it."

"No. No, not a problem child." Jill looked around and said, "His daughter's name is Whitney. Mr Cater wants a sitter/companion for her for the next few weeks."

"A long-term job. That's good." Sunny leaned over and fished for the record book.

"She's twelve," said Jill.

That stopped us.

"Twelve?" I asked. "She's almost our age!"

"She's been attending a special school with a summer programme, but she's leaving the summer programme because she's about to be moved out of her old school and into the state school system. Her parents have found a day camp for Whitney and they're going to take off alternate mornings for the next few weeks until the camp begins. But they need a sitter for the afternoons.'

Jill paused, then added, "Whitney has Down's syndrome."

There was a little silence, then Maggie

said, "Like Corky, right? In that TV show."

"Yes," said Jill.

"OK," said Sunny. "It's a long job. Does anybody want to take on the whole thing, every afternoon? Or do we want to split it up?"

"I'll take it," I said. "Unless someone else. . . ?"

Maggie said, "I would, but I can't do the whole thing. Having just one person on the job might be easier. But I'd like to be counted as your substitute if you can't make it one day or something."

"OK," said Sunny, handing the record book to me.

I took it and Jill handed me the phone number and Mr Cater's name.

I called Mr Cater back at his office.

"Good," he said. "Let me write that down in my book. Dawn Schafer." He gave me the details and concluded. "Whitney will be pleased, I think. We've decided to tell her you're a new friend, rather than a babysitter. She feels she doesn't need a babysitter, especially now that she's graduating to state school."

"Great," I said. "I'll see you then."

I rang off, intrigued and pleased with my new job and with the prospect of steady work for several weeks to come.

3rd CHAPTER

The Caters didn't live far from our house, so I walked there the first afternoon I was supposed to babysit for Whitney.

Babysit? No, that wasn't exactly the right word. I had talked to both Mr and Mrs Cater several times since accepting the job and although I hadn't actually met them, I felt as if I knew them, and Whitney, too.

I admit, I had been rather worried at first, even though the job had intrigued me. I had never met anyone with Down's syndrome before and I wasn't sure quite what to expect. I didn't think it would be the same as the babysitting job Kristy had had, back in Stoneybrook, with an autistic girl called Susan, who never spoke or even seemed to pay attention to what was going on around her. (Although she could play just about any piece of music on the piano after hearing it only once.) Some specialists thought Susan was retarded, although no one was sure. And no one, not even the specialists, knew what had caused Susan's disability.

No one knows why children with Down's syndrome are born the way they are, either, according to Mr Cater.

"It's a congenital defect," he said. "That means it develops before birth. It's caused by a chromosome abnormality, the appearance of a certain chromosome three times instead of twice in some or all of the cells. No one knows why it happens."

"Oh," I said. At that point, I didn't understand much more than I had before.

Mr Cater went on. "Practically speaking, it means that Whitney is retarded. She's not very retarded. Many people with Down's syndrome aren't. And she doesn't have any extreme manifestations of physical traits commonly associated with Down's syndrome, such as retarded growth or impaired coordination, or thank God, a heart condition. It's one of the reasons we feel that Whitney will be able to join the educational mainstream fairly easily, relatively speaking. Of course, she'll continue to take some special courses, and to work with specialists, like her speech therapist."

"Oh," I said again. I understood a little more of what Mr Cater had said this time, but I didn't know how to ask him what I really wanted to find out: what was Whitney like?

I smiled as I walked down the street, remembering what had happened next. Mr Cater had cleared his throat and said, "Perhaps you should speak to Annette. My wife. I'll ask her to ring you when she gets home from work."

Mrs Cater had called soon after. What she told me had been less technical and more specific.

"Whitney is so excited about going to a new school," she'd said, straight away. "And so excited about meeting a new friend."

"About that. The new friend story," I'd said. "Are you sure that's what you want to tell her?" Somehow, the idea made me uncomfortable. I'd never lied to anyone I'd sat for before.

"That's what we *have* told her. That you're a new friend. As my husband may have explained to you, Whitney's pride would be hurt if we told her we'd hired a babysitter. After all, she's twelve years old!" Mrs Cater laughed.

"I can understand *that*," I said, remembering how hard some of us (such as Mary Anne) had worked to convince our parents that we weren't little kids any more, that we could make decisions on our own and handle more grown-up responsibility. But even though I could understand, I wanted to say more. However, Mrs Cater didn't give me a chance.

"Good," she said emphatically. "Anyway, Whitney is easy-going. She likes laughing. She's a good listener. She's very sympathetic and sensitive to others' moods. She's friendly and outgoing and although she's retarded, she's only mildly retarded. All in all, I don't think you'll find her too different from any of your other babysitting charges."

"OK," I said. "Sounds great."

We had worked out the details of my first visit, and rung off.

Oops! I'd been so busy thinking that I'd almost walked right past the Caters' house. I backtracked a few steps, hoping no one was watching, and made my way to the front door. The Caters opened the door almost as soon as I'd knocked.

"Hello," I said. "I'm Dawn Schafer from the We Love Kids Club."

"Of course," said the woman. "I'm

Annette Cater and this is my husband, James."

"Hello, Mrs Cater. Hello, Mr Cater."

"Come in," said Mrs Cater, stepping back.

I stepped in, then followed the Caters down a spacious hallway to a large sunny room at the back of the house.

"Whitney is folding up her laundry and putting it away," explained Mrs Cater. "She'll be here in a minute. I told her it was important to have a tidy room for her guest."

"Oh," I said, trying to remember the last time I'd tidied up my room when Sunny or anyone had come over.

"I'm going in to my office this afternoon," said Mrs Cater. "James is here for his lunch hour, so we'll both be leaving shortly. There is a list over by the phone of our office numbers, emergency numbers and neighbours' names and numbers if anything should come up."

"Great," I said. We babysitters love it when parents are prepared like that. Surprisingly, not all parents always are. I was about to ask if Whitney had any rules I should know about, or any special foods she should or shouldn't eat, allergies or medications I should know about, but Mr Cater beat me to it.

30

"Whitney is prone to ear infections," he said. "She has to wear special ear plugs when she goes swimming and put drops in before and after. Other than that, she has no allergies or anything that you need to worry about." He paused, then smiled. "Except she does have a sweet tooth."

I was about to ask if Whitney had any games or special things she liked to do, but Mrs Cater looked past me towards the door and said brightly, "Whitney. Here's Dawn. She's come to keep you company this afternoon while we're at work."

I stood up and turned around to see a short, somewhat stocky girl standing in the doorway. She had straight brown hair and brown eyes that seemed to slant slightly at the corners. Her face was round and she had a short nose. As she stood there looking at me, she didn't change expression at all.

I smiled. "Hi, Whitney."

Whitney's face immediately broke into a wide grin and she said, "Hi, Dawn! That's a pretty name."

"Thank you," I said. Whitney's voice was low, almost hoarse, and she spoke carefully.

Whitney came towards me and held out her hand. "How do you do?" she asked.

Smiling inwardly at this lesson in

31

manners that Whitney was so obviously practising, I took her hand. "Fine, thank you. How are you?"

"Fine, thank you," said Whitney. Then she burst out, "I want earrings, too."

I could tell the Caters had heard that before. "When the right time comes, dear," said Mr Cater, standing up. He bent to kiss the top of Whitney's head. "Your mother and I are going to work while Dawn stays here. We'll be back at six."

"Goodbye," said Whitney. She was staring intently at my ears. Then she said triumphantly, "You've got *four* earrings, Dawn. I want four earrings."

"I'm thirteen," I said quickly. "Maybe when you're my age, you can get earrings."

Mrs Cater smiled and patted her daughter's shoulder. "See you in a little while, Whitney. There's juice in the fridge if you want something to drink, Dawn. And help yourself to whatever you want in the kitchen. But don't let Whitney spoil her appetite for dinner."

I was worried for a moment that Mrs Cater's instructions would sound too much like she was leaving me in charge, like a babysitter, but Whitney didn't seem to notice. She looked up at her parents and said, "Goodbye, Mum. Goodbye, Dad."

A few minutes later, the Caters were gone.

"What a beautiful day," I said. "What do you want to do?"

In answer, Whitney caught my hand and pulled me out into the hall.

"Where are we going, Whitney?" I asked.

"To my room," explained Whitney. "It's *tidy*."

"That's great. I'm not too good about tidying up my room. But if *I'm* bad, you should see my brother Jeff! The messes he makes are *dreadful*. My father just closes the door sometimes and says as long as he can't smell anything, he's assuming it's OK."

Whitney nodded, almost absent-mindedly, and flung the door of her room open proudly. "Look!" she said.

I wasn't sure what I expected to see, but it was a typical girl's room, decorated in green and white and soft peach. A big canopy bed stood in the middle of the room with a patchwork quilt across the foot. A wide desk with a chair was by the window, and next to it was a comfortable-looking armchair. Book-shelves lined one wall and on the other wall was a big poster of seals cavorting in the ocean.

"You like the water," I said, remembering what Mr Cater had said.

"I'm a good swimmer," answered Whitney. "See?" She pointed to the bookshelves and I realized that many of the shelves held trophies.

"Wow!" I said. "Did you win all these?"

Whitney nodded. "At my school. We have swimming galas every year."

"That's great, Whitney!" I said.

"Do you like swimming?" asked Whitney.

"I certainly do," I answered. "And surfing."

Whitney's eyes lit up. "In the sea?" She thought for a minute, then said. "Great!"

I laughed.

Whitney laughed, too. Then she squatted down and pulled a stack of magazines out from the bottom of her bookshelf.

"What's that?" I asked.

"Magazines. M-my mother's," explained Whitney.

I sat down on the floor and Whitney straightened her legs out slowly and sat next to me. She opened the magazines and pointed to a picture of Keanu Reeves.

"He's cute."

"Yes," I agreed. "Very."

"Do you think he's cute?"

"Yep. But I like him better." I pointed to the photo of another star. Whitney studied him seriously, her head turned to one side and her tongue sticking out slightly from between her lips.

Then she said, "No. I like Keanu better."

"Well, I like what he's wearing better," I said.

Whitney nodded and turned the page. She studied the picture for a moment and then said, "*He's* got earrings, too."

I laughed and shook my head. "Soon you'll have them, too. Your parents just want you to be more grown-up."

"I *am* grown-up!" Whitney exclaimed.

"Yes, but parents never believe you are. You have to show them," I said.

Whitney thought for a moment, then nodded. Then she said, "Have you got a boyfriend?"

"No. Not at the moment. Have you?" I asked.

Whitney giggled and put her hand over her mouth. "No. Not yet." Her eyes lit on my rucksack, which I'd dropped on the floor next to me.

"Have you got any magazines in there?" she asked, pointing.

"No. It's mostly empty," I answered.

"May I look inside?"

"OK," I said, sliding the rucksack over to her. She opened it and my string shopping bag fell out.

"What's this?" she asked.

"It's a string bag," I said. "I carry it with me wherever I go so that if I buy anything, I can put it in there instead of in a plastic bag. Plastic bags are bad for the environment."

Whitney nodded, but her attention had been caught by something else. "Ooh, make-up!" She pulled out a tube of clear pink sunscreen lip gloss and held it up admiringly. "May I try it on, Dawn? Please?"

"Of course," I said.

Whitney scrambled to her feet and went over to the small mirror hanging above her chest of drawers. She opened the lip gloss with great care. Drawing her eyebrows together in a frown, she leaned forward and meticulously outlined her lips with the gloss.

"It looks nice," I said, coming to stand beside her. Our two faces looked back at us from the mirror: mine tanned, with a faint dusting of freckles, my hair straight and white-blonde on either side of my face, Whitney's face pale and round with her short dark hair and flat, immobile features. But then she smiled and I didn't think she looked so expressionless after all. Or so different.

I decided it was like getting to know anybody new. At first, new people look strange because, well, they're strangers. But after that you know them and then they just look like themselves.

"Nice," repeated Whitney. She nodded in satisfaction, closed the tube of gloss with equal care and handed it ceremoniously back to me. "Thank you, Dawn."

"You're welcome," I said. I walked over to my rucksack and put the gloss back in and sat down. "So, what else do you do besides swim? Have you got other favourite sports? Or hobbies?"

Whitney thought for a moment, then said, "I like animals. I like bears. And seals. I want to get a job, too. I'd like to babysit and earn money of my own."

"That's what I do to earn money," I said. "Some friends of mine and I have our own babysitting business, the We Love Kids Club."

"Really? Do you earn lots of money?"

"Well, not exactly," I answered. "But we do a lot of work. Being a good baby-sitter is a big responsibility. I've even gone to classes to learn how to be a better baby-sitter."

Whitney asked me what seemed like a

million questions about my job. We sat on her floor and laughed and talked until I heard the front door open and Mr Cater's voice call, "Whitney? Dawn?"

I went home feeling pretty good. Whitney was nice. And fun. And funny. I'd enjoyed this job a lot, and I was looking forward to seeing Whitney again the next afternoon.

4th
CHAPTER

"I don't like that colour." Whitney held a magazine up for me to inspect. A boy in an olive green T-shirt and a black zebra-print jacket smiled out at us from the page. Whitney pointed to the model's shirt.

"Yes," I said. "He's cute, but that colour green is awful. At least, it would look terrible on me. I look better in summer colours."

Whitney switched her attention from the model to me. "Summer colours?" she asked.

"Yes. You know, the colours you usually see in the summer: bright blue skies, bright yellow sun. Those are the colours that look best on me. But other people look better in colours from other seasons of the year. I've got a friend in

Connecticut, Mallory, and she's got red hair and pale skin and freckles. She looks really good in autumn colours, like the autumn leaf colours. You know, orange-red and gold. Like that."

Whitney frowned. Then she said, "What colours am I?"

I studied her for a moment, her brown eyes and dark hair. Then I said, "Maybe spring. Spring green and all the colours of the spring flowers."

"I like that," said Whitney. "Spring. Spring colours. You are summer and I am spring."

"Yes," I said, grinning.

Whitney flipped through a couple more magazines, talking about the different colours. It was interesting to look at magazines that way, as if I were learning different colours in a whole new way. I was used to helping very young babysitting charges work on learning their colours. I would say, "What colour is the apple? What colour is the sky?" But I'd never done anything quite like this before.

Soon we'd gone through a whole stack of magazines. I pulled out a couple more from Whitney's huge stack, but she pushed them to one side and shook her head impatiently.

"I'm tired of magazines," she said.

I thought for a moment of the Kid-Kits we use in the BSC back in Connecticut. Kid-Kits (another brilliant Kristy invention) are boxes that we take on some of our babysitting jobs. Inside the boxes are books and puzzles and toys, not necessarily new things, but things that are new to the kids we're looking after. They're always fascinated by the contents of the Kid-Kits and are delighted to be allowed to play with the "new" stuff inside.

But a Kid-Kit wouldn't work for Whitney. Even if the contents did interest her, she'd probably feel it was too babyish. Also, I didn't want to do anything that might make her think I was babysitting for her.

"Do you like playing games?" I asked.

Whitney looked wary. "Sometimes. But at school when we play games, sometimes it means we have to pick up our toys and help tidy up the room."

I had to laugh. "Yes. Don't you hate it when teachers try to trick you like that?"

Whitney nodded emphatically. "They should just say, 'Will you please pick everything up from the floor?'"

I suddenly remembered that Sunny was sitting for Clover and Daffodil Austin, who lived next door to me.

"Hey, Whitney, remember the job I

41

told you about? The one I have babysitting as a member of the We Love Kids Club?"

"Yes! Babysitting. I want to babysit," said Whitney.

"Right. Well, a friend of mine, Sunny, has got a babysitting job near here too— er—today. Right now, in fact. We could go and visit her at work."

Nodding excitedly, Whitney said, "Yes. Let's do that."

Phew! She hadn't noticed my slip-up, when I referred to Sunny having a babysitting job, *too*. I stood up and reached down to pull Whitney to her feet. She lost her balance a little and she nearly pulled me over.

"Oops!" I said, staggering and regaining my balance.

"Oops!" repeated Whitney.

I left a note with Mr and Mrs Cater in case they came home early (although I didn't think that they would), and Whitney and I set out for the Austins'.

Since we had another perfect day, complete with all the best colours of summer, from amazing sky blue to sunshine gold, I wasn't surprised when we reached the Austins' to find the girls in their swimsuits, playing with hoses and sprinklers. Clover was clutching a big flower that

42

squirted water and chasing Daffodil through the sprinklers shooting water at her. "I'm raining flowers, I'm raining flowers!" Clover was shouting. Although she was soaking wet like her sister, Daffodil was shrieking every time Clover sprayed her.

Daffodil is nine and Clover is six, but Clover is the Austin you notice first. She lives at the top of her lungs, sort of like Karen, Kristy's little sister. She saw me and shouted, "DAWN!"

Whitney's eyes widened and I laughed. "Hi, Clover! Hi, Daffodil." Daffodil, still running away from Clover, waved her arms in what might have been a greeting as Whitney and I strolled over to join Sunny, who was watching from the *extreme* edge of the water fight.

"Sunny," I said. "Hi. This is Whitney. I told her about the We Love Kids Club and she wanted to come with me to visit you while you work."

I'd already told Sunny and the others that my babysitting job with Whitney was undercover, so I knew Sunny wouldn't give me away.

Whitney held out her hand. After a moment, Sunny took it and gave it a little shake.

"It's nice to meet you, Sunny," said

Whitney, in the same careful, practised way she'd spoken when she'd met me.

Sunny paused, then said, "I'm glad to meet you, too, Whitney. Do you want to join Clover and Daffodil?"

"Yes!" exclaimed Whitney instantly.

"Dawn?" said Sunny. *I* knew she was asking me if it was all right for Whitney to join in, but Whitney didn't.

"You'll play, too, won't you, Dawn? Do you want to?"

I hesitated. As Whitney's "friend" there was no reason for me not to join in the sprinkler frolics, but as the person responsible for her, I didn't know if it was such a good idea.

Luckily, Sunny came to my rescue. "If Dawn doesn't want to, she could keep me company."

"OK," said Whitney. "I need my swimsuit." She turned back towards her house.

"Whitney, wait," I said. To Sunny, I said, "See you in a few minutes."

"We'll be here," Sunny assured me.

I had to hurry to keep up with Whitney as she went back home. I changed the note to the Caters, telling them where we were and what we were doing, while Whitney changed into her swimsuit. A few minutes later, she came out wearing a bathing cap, and a big shirt that almost reached her knees. She was carrying a towel and a small plastic box in her hand.

"Shoes?" I said, pointing.

"Oh. Thank you, Dawn. I almost forgot."

She came back a minute later wearing trainers.

"What have you got in there?" I asked, indicating the plastic box in her left hand.

"Ear plugs," said Whitney. "They're special ear plugs. Water makes my ears hurt sometimes and I have to take medicine. But if I wear these every time I swim, then my ears don't hurt and I don't have to take medicine."

"Ear infections," I said, remembering what Mr Cater had said.

"That's right," said Whitney, pleased that I'd "guessed".

"Have you got drops, too, to put in before and after?"

Whitney looked at me in surprise and I said, "When you're a babysitter, you have to know these things."

"Yes. But I'm not swimming. Do I need the drops?"

"Better safe than sorry," I said. Mrs Cater had told me the drops were in the downstairs bathroom cabinet. "I'll get them," I said, and hurried away.

Whitney was waiting impatiently when I reached the front porch. "Come *on*, Dawn," she said.

"Coming, coming," I said, laughing.

When we got back to the Austins', Whitney carefully put her ear drops in, then her ear plugs, then folded her towel, lined her trainers up next to it, gave the ear drops back to me, and slid the ear plug container into the toe of one of the trainers. Then she turned and waved wildly.

I ducked. "Whoa, Whitney!"

"I'm here," she called to Clover and Daffodil, and waded into the sprinklers.

"Eek!" shrieked Daffodil, who was now holding the hose to keep Clover at bay. She turned and splashed Whitney and Clover with it.

Whitney put her hands over her head as if she were about to dive headfirst into a swimming pool and dived down the spray of water.

"I'm a hose fish!" cried Whitney.

"A hose fish, a hose fish!" screamed Clover, imitating Whitney, and adding her own wiggly side-to-side movements. She "swam" back towards her sister from the other side.

"EEEEEEK!" Daffodil cried again,

flinging down the hose and taking off.

Clover grabbed the hose and turned it on Daffodil and Whitney, who charged away, laughing.

If I'd had any worries about how Clover and Daffodil would take to the "new kid", they'd just been washed away.

"Wow!" Sunny said. She sat down on the steps and sprawled out to turn her face up to the sun. "Where do they get so much energy?"

"Pretty amazing," I agreed, imitating Sunny's example.

"Flower fish!" cried Whitney, who'd got hold of the hose and was holding it straight up in the air. Clover and Daffodil immediately began to twirl around, making fluttery motions with their hands.

"Sunny, come and play," panted Clover, twirling up close and spraying us with water.

"Hey, flower fish, you're watering *me*!" said Sunny, laughing.

"Don't you want to play?" asked Clover, still spinning.

"Thank you, but no thanks. I'll keep Dawn company, OK?"

Clover shrugged and spun away.

We sat in the sun watching the dance of the water flowers for most of the afternoon. The three girls couldn't have been happier.

At last Sunny stood up and walked over to the taps. "Time for a snack!" she called and turned the water off.

The three, soaking wet, splashed around in the puddles for a moment longer, then came tumbling across the lawn in a spray of water.

"Towels over here," I said.

"Dry yourselves," Sunny said, "and we'll all go and see about something good to eat."

The kitchen yielded plenty of great food: vegetable crisps and yogurt dip, oatmeal raisin biscuits, and a slice of watermelon. More than enough food for all of us, even those of us with a huge appetite from lawn swimming, right?

Wrong. Clover and Daffodil both took one look at the watermelon and made a grab for it.

"Mine!" said Clover.

"I saw it first," Daffodil said, her voice rising.

"You did not!"

"I did!"

"Er, girls. . ." I said.

"Hey, you two," began Sunny.

Whitney reached out and drew the

watermelon back across the table to the middle.

"You should cut the watermelon in half," she said slowly. "You should cut it, Daffodil. Then . . . then Clover gets to choose first. That's fair." She nodded emphatically.

I looked at Sunny. Sunny looked at me. We both looked at the two sisters.

Watermelon fight averted.

"OK," said Daffodil, picking up the knife. She cut the watermelon very, very carefully in half, making sure that the pieces were exactly even, while Clover watched closely.

Then, after much consideration, Clover chose one of the two identical pieces of watermelon and the two settled back with their treat.

Whitney reached for the oatmeal raisin biscuits and Sunny and I made a nice-sized dent in the vegetable crisps (of course).

The afternoon ended peacefully, and two tired but happy girls waved enthusiastically as Whitney and I left.

"Come back soon," called Clover.

"Soon!" echoed Daffodil.

"That was fun," said Whitney.

"Yes, it was. You were great with Clover and Daffodil." I had been really, truly impressed with Whitney's skill with the two girls, and with her own responsible behaviour in wearing the ear plugs and keeping them in.

Whitney ducked her head a little and nodded, smiling. "They're nice. Sunny's nice. She's a good babysitter."

"And a good friend," I said, smiling at the memory of Sunny propped back on her elbows in the sun.

"Is Sunny your best friend?" Whitney asked.

"One of them," I said.

We'd reached the last crossroads before Whitney's street. It had got much busier with the after-work traffic.

Whitney, who'd been about half a step ahead of me, stopped so abruptly that I bumped into her.

"Whitney?" I said.

Whitney stepped sideways. Then stepped forward tentatively. A car whizzed by and slammed on its brakes as the light turned to amber. Whitney leaped back and began to rock nervously from one foot to the other.

I looked both ways. The cars had stopped.

"Come on," I said.

Whitney rocked to and fro. "I don't know," she said. "I don't know."

"Whitney?"

"So many cars," said Whitney. "I don't know."

Whitney suddenly sounded very, very young.

"Whitney," I said gently. "It's OK." I reached for her hand, then realized that she might think I was treating her like a baby. So I slid my arm through hers.

"Let's walk across together, OK?"

Whitney stopped rocking to and fro and some of the panic left her eyes. She looked at me, then at the line of stopped cars.

"O-OK, Dawn."

We stepped off the kerb and walked across the street together.

"Red makes the cars stop, and lets the people walk across," said Whitney softly as we got to the other side.

"That's right," I said.

"Yes," said Whitney, her panic now completely forgotten. She smiled at me trustingly. "Can we go and see Clover and Daffodil again soon?"

"Yes," I said. "And we'll have a great afternoon tomorrow, too."

"OK," said Whitney.

I couldn't help but think, as we went back to Whitney's house, how different she was from anyone I'd ever known—so grown-up in so many ways, and so very young in others.

Then I had to laugh at myself. How different, after all, was that from any of us? It was just that, for Whitney, the grown-up part of her mind could only grow up so much. But for most of the rest of us, we had to keep growing up whether we liked it or not.

5th CHAPTER

Wednesday

Seven kids who get along seem like a lot fewer than seven kids who don't get along, if you know what I mean, Claud.

That's the truth, Stacey. And who can forget how much the Barretts and the Dewits didn't get along? But now they are getting along just greeeattt!

So be prepared, Dawn, we're going to write and tell you all about what great baby-sitters Claudia and I are!

Stacey and Claudia were in charge of seven kids for the evening: the three Barretts—eight-year-old Buddy, five-year-old Suzi, and their baby sister Marnie—and the four DeWitts—eight-year-old Lindsey, six-year-old Taylor, four-year-old Madeleine, and two-year-old Ryan.

As Mr Franklin DeWitt, the man Mrs Barrett has been dating, is a very punctual and organized person, he got to the Barretts' front door with his four kids at the same time as Stacey and Claudia.

"Hi, everyone," said Stacey.

"Allow me," said Franklin, and he reached out and rang the doorbell and then made a sort of bow in Stacey and Claudia's direction. All the DeWitt kids giggled and Franklin grinned, obviously pleased with his little joke. He was clearly in a very good mood.

Mrs Barrett answered the door and smiled radiantly at Franklin. She's someone who is, well, organizationally different, but she always manages to look well groomed and that night was no exception. If Franklin looked handsome in his suit and tie, Mrs Barrett looked like a model in her silk dress and gold earrings (one of which she was putting on as she opened the door) and upswept hair.

"There you are," she cried, as if it was

all a huge, wonderful surprise to find Franklin, four kids, and two babysitters on her front porch. "Come in, come in."

Ryan suddenly got shy, and sidled into the house.

Stacey bent over and scooped him up. "Why don't I give you a piggy-back, Ryan? How would you like that?"

Ryan nodded, and Stacey boosted him on to her back while Mrs Barrett grabbed her bag and gave Stacey and Claudia last-minute instructions.

"Dinner is —" said Mrs Barrett and waved her hand in the direction of the kitchen.

"Potluck?" supplied Franklin, smiling. "A smorgasbord? Everything sandwiches?"

"Exactly!" Mrs Barrett beamed at him and seemed to forget that anyone else was standing in the hall except Franklin and her.

Claudia cleared her throat. "Great. Er, approximately what time will you. . ."

"Early," said Franklin, smiling at Mrs Barrett the same way. "No later than eight. It's just a cocktail party. A business thing, really."

"Great," said Claudia again.

No one moved for a moment. Then

Stacey said, "So, Mrs Barrett, Mr DeWitt, have a good time."

That broke the spell, at least for the moment. Mrs Barrett, her cheeks a little pink, nodded and said, "Thank you."

"We will," said Franklin, still looking at Mrs Barrett. He made the same sort of funny little bow he'd made on the porch but no one giggled. When he held out his arm, Mrs Barrett took it and sort of floated out of the door with him.

"What's a smorgasbord?" asked Lindsey DeWitt. "Is it good?"

"Well, it's sort of potluck, I suppose," said Claudia.

"What's a potluck?" asked Suzi.

"That's when the guests who go to a party each bring a special dish. That's a potluck supper."

"Oh," said Suzi.

"A smorgasbord is more like all kinds of different foods that people can pick and choose to eat from. You put it out on a table and. . ."

"A cafeteria!" exclaimed Buddy.

"Sort of like that, too," said Stacey. "Only I think you can go back as many times as you want and get all kinds of different things."

"Can we have smorgas . . . smorgas . . . potluck?" asked Taylor DeWitt.

Stacey thought for a moment. It was a beautiful summer evening, clear and not too warm. "It would be nice to do something outside," she said.

"What about a smorgasbord picnic?" suggested Claudia. "We'll put everything out on the table here and make up a picnic from it and then take it to the park and play games and have a picnic. A smorgaspic!"

"A smorgaspic!" cried Taylor.

Marnie Barrett clapped her hands together.

Soon the seven kids were running to and fro in the kitchen, lining things up on the kitchen table.

"Ketchup, pickles, tuna salad," chanted Buddy, leaning forward to look in the fridge.

"Hands off!" said Lindsey behind him and Ryan reached in and grabbed the ketchup and the pickles and the tuna salad, one at a time and passed them back to Lindsey, who put them on the table.

"Bread," cried Taylor as he emerged from the pantry, holding a loaf of wholewheat bread aloft.

"Salami, jam and stinky cheese," Buddy went on.

"Ugh! Stinky cheese!" shouted Suzi. She took the package, labelled *Gorgon-*

zola, out of Lindsey's hand and sniffed it, then frowned. "It doesn't stink."

Lindsey laughed and peeled back a corner of the wrapper. "Now smell," she said.

Suzi leaned over and sniffed again, then shrieked delightedly, "Ugh! Ugh! Stinky, stinky!"

"Stinky!" cried Marnie, joining in the excitement.

"Inky," whispered Ryan, who'd been dropping the paper napkins one by one into a basket Claudia had given him.

When the table couldn't hold any more food, the seven kids set to work making a smorgaspic, with a little help from Claudia and Stacey.

They loaded the picnic into Suzi's truck and took turns pulling it to the park, with Suzi and Taylor pulling together for their turn.

It was hard to believe these were the same kids who once got along so badly they had to be separated when people babysat for them together. That had been back when they first met, just after Mrs Barrett and Franklin had started going out. But once they got used to the idea of their respective parents seeing each other, and once Mrs Barrett and Mr DeWitt stopped trying so hard to make everybody like everybody, and just let people be themselves (with a little help from the members of the BSC, world-class babysitters), the seven kids now got along OK.

They even seemed to share the same bizarre taste in food, as Stacey and Claudia discovered at the park.

After an energetic game of freeze tag and a very funny game of pass the egg on the spoon (Stacey had brought along a couple of hard-boiled eggs from the fridge, which were completely cracked and squashed by the time the game was over), the smorgaspic got underway.

Stacey had packed an apple and a container of leftover rice and black beans, because she has to be careful about what she eats. It was a good thing she had, because the smorgaspic had a really stunning assortment of food. It even stunned Claudia, who picked up what she thought was a tuna salad sandwich and took a big bite.

"W-what *is* this?" she gasped, making a hideous face.

"Claudia?" asked Stacey. "Are you all right?"

Claudia peeled the top of the sandwich back while the Barretts and the DeWitts burst into laughter. "Jaffa cakes!" cried

Claudia. "Who put crushed Jaffa cakes on my sandwich?"

Taylor reached out and took the sandwich. "I invented it," he said. He took a big bite and said, "I like it."

"Can I try it?" asked Suzi. She took a bite, chewed thoughtfully for a minute, then said, "I like it, too."

Claudia fished around and found a plain tuna sandwich. But among the sandwiches she and Stacey watched the Barretts and the DeWitts eat and share with each other with gusto, apart from the tuna salad and Jaffa cakes were peanut butter and crisps, coleslaw and salami, and grape jelly and Cheddar cheese.

As they trudged home from the park, feeling full up and tired, Stacey said, "I hope they won't get stomach aches."

Claudia shuddered. "I thought I was a junk food fanatic, but this group has got me beat. Still, your food just gets all mixed together in your stomach anyway."

"Thanks for saying that, Claudia," said Stacey, making a face of her own.

After all the games and the smorgaspic, Marnie went to bed without any fuss, and since Ryan was looking rather sleepy himself, they tucked him into Buddy's bed.

Then they took turns reading an old book that Buddy had found on one of the bookshelves: *Cheaper By the Dozen*, about a family with twelve kids in it. It was rather old fashioned, but it was funny, too.

Not long after that, Mrs Barrett and Franklin got back. Mrs Barrett was holding on to Franklin's arm just as she had been when they left. And she was still staring at him in that same mesmerized way, only her cheeks were very pink. She was practically glowing, and so was Franklin.

"Was it fun?" asked Claudia, as Mrs Barrett was paying them.

"What? Oh, the party. Oh, it was *wonderful*," breathed Mrs Barrett. The two adults exchanged a long look.

Franklin said, "Truly wonderful. The most special night of my life."

"Oh. Well, great," said Stacey. She grabbed Claudia's elbow and steered her out of the door.

"I wonder what's going on?" said Claudia.

"I don't know, but something's up," said Stacey. "Oh, well, at least the days of the Barrett/DeWitt feud are over."

"For ever," agreed Claudia.

"And ever," said Stacey.

6th CHAPTER

"Hello, hello, hel-lo!" My father bounded through the door of the family room.

I looked at him. He was smiling. Was this a good sign or a bad sign? He'd just got back from another one of his first dates. "Clarice Dubina," he'd said over his shoulder as he'd rushed out to his date earlier in the evening. "More later."

I suppose later had arrived. I pointed the remote control at the television and clicked it off.

"Hi, Dad," I said. "What's up?"

"Why did the lobster move to a bigger house?" asked my father.

"Is this a Jeff joke?" I asked.

Jeff, who was sprawled on the floor, shook his head. "Nope," he said.

"You'll like it, Jeff. Go on, why did the lobster move to a bigger house."

"I give up," I said immediately. "Why?"

Jeff took longer. His professional reputation as a comedian was at stake. But at last he too said, "I give up."

"Because he had 'clawstrophobia'! Get it? Claustrophobia."

I managed to smile. "I get it, Dad."

Jeff gave a big horse laugh. "That's great, Dad! Where did you hear that one?"

"Our waiter at the restaurant tonight."

I had a sudden flash of inspiration. "Did you go to the Ocean Inn for dinner?" The Ocean Inn was a local seafood house, really plain inside, but heaps of seafood on every plate.

And waiters who were planning to be comedians, obviously.

Dad nodded and beamed as if I'd got the right answer on a quiz show. "It was great," he said. "Terrific. I like someone who can match me oyster for oyster."

"You ate *raw* oysters?" Jeff grabbed his throat and let his head drop to one side.

"Yep. Wait and see, Jeff. You'll try them one day and like them, too."

I didn't want to clutch my throat and act like Jeff, but I admit, the idea of *ever* letting a slimy, raw oyster touch my lips made me go "ick" inside. But I smiled and said (bravely), "Sounds like fun, Dad."

"It was. It definitely was. So . . ."

"Time for the family date," I finished.

Dad nodded. "A fair is coming to town this weekend. Clarice thought it might be a fun outing for all of us."

"A fair?" Jeff recovered from his imaginary oyster binge to sit up and protest. "That's for little kids!" But from the sparkle in his eyes, I could tell he was hooked on the idea.

"Little kids!" My father pretended to be indignant. "I'm not a little kid and I love fairs. The rides, the games, the candyfloss. . ."

"The popcorn," I put in quickly. (Ugh! Oysters and candyfloss in one conversation.) "The people. I like fairs too, Dad."

"Well," Jeff said. "OK. If you two really want to go, I suppose I could come too."

"Great," said my father. "The fair on Saturday it is. This is going to be *fun*."

Did I mention that my father is one of those weird eternal optimists?

The fair was a disaster.

We picked up Clarice and my heart sank when she slid into the car, turned to look at Jeff and me sitting in the back seat, and said, "So these are the children. They're a great looking pair, Schaf."

Schaf? *Schaf?* Jeff and I exchanged glances, but then I thought, hey, what's in a nickname? Look at mine.

"Hi," I said, deciding to ignore the nickname and the fact that she'd just called me and Jeff children. "I'm Dawn and this is Jeff."

Jeff didn't say anything. I elbowed him. Hard.

"Owww!" cried Jeff.

"Now, children, no fighting. We'll be there in just a few minutes, won't we, Schaf?" Clarice gave us a big, big smile and turned back to my father.

Children. She'd done it again. Next to me, Jeff folded his arms. I didn't have to look at him to know that his eyes were narrowed and his lower lip was sticking out. He had jumped, quick as a flash, into one of his stubborn moods. It didn't bode well for the evening.

I was right.

Bright lights, lots of noise, the smell of popcorn and candyfloss, the grind of the motors, and the shrieks of the people on the rides, the clanging of bells and whistles and sirens at all the games, enormous silly stuffed animals—the fair had everything it was supposed to have.

Except three Schafers and one Clarice having a good time.

Clarice started talking the moment we arrived and she didn't stop the whole time, pointing things out to us, grabbing our arms and squeezing our shoulders for emphasis, telling Schaf that the children would love this ride or that.

"Look," she exclaimed. She squeezed my father's arm, my shoulder, and ruffled Jeff's hair before he could duck out of the way. "Bumper cars!"

"Boring," said Jeff.

"Silly boy!" cried Clarice. "Come on, Schaf, let's show the children we old people can still do the bump!" Clarice charged up to the ticket booth with our father in tow and a few minutes later we were seated in our respective bumper cars.

I looked over at Jeff. He was looking at Clarice. It didn't take a rocket scientist to work out what would happen next.

Wham! Jeff ploughed into the side of Clarice's bumper car.

She gave a little shriek of laughter and began to turn her wheel frantically. But Jeff didn't give her a chance. "Wham! Wham!" Clarice's car spun round and round. "Wham!"

Clarice's mouth opened, but before she could laugh, Jeff got her again.

Whack! Someone jolted into me and I lost sight of the two of them, and spent the rest of the time maintaining my own bumper car defence. But I was pretty sure that no one attacked me as relentlessly as Jeff attacked Clarice.

I had to give Clarice credit, though. She smiled brightly as we climbed out of our cars, and said, as if she hadn't even noticed Jeff's all-out attack, "Now, wasn't that fun?"

"Terrific," said Jeff. "Let's do it again."

"Not now, Jeff," said our father quickly. Dad had noticed even if Clarice hadn't.

Jeff accepted that easily. Too easily. The next minute he was pointing at a booth where giant lime green pandas dangled from the rafters. "Look, Dawn! You remember how you've always tried and tried to win one of those? Let's try again!"

"*What?*" Before I could protest or say Jeff was crazy, Clarice had said, "Oh, Dawn, really? Well, let's see what we can do about getting you the toy of your dreams."

"Toy?" I said. "But. . ."

Too late. Clarice had already marched over to the booth and plonked down her money for three balls to knock over a stack of three pins.

She missed.

She missed again.

"That's OK," I said. "Really."

"No, no, no," said Clarice.

I resigned myself to the idea of wandering the fair for the rest of the night lugging a green panda around. Maybe I could give it to Whitney, I thought. Or to Clover or Daffodil.

Unfortunately, Clarice's aim was terrible. She tried and tried and tried, but she couldn't win. And Jeff, the little rat, kept encouraging her, looking over his shoulder to say things like, "Don't worry, Dawn. She'll get it this time."

Eventually my father cleared his throat. "Tell you what, next time I see a panda in a shop, I'll buy you one, Dawn."

Just at that moment, Clarice succeeded. "Ha!" she cried. "There, Schaf." She seized the panda from the grinning stall-holder and bestowed it on me.

"Thanks," I said weakly. I was going to get Jeff for this!

"No problem, kiddo," Clarice said.

"Time for—" our father began.

"Candyfloss! I haven't had that in years. Since I was a child," Clarice said. "I remember I used to make myself positively *sick* on candyfloss. Do you children do that?"

"How about popcorn, Dad?" I said quickly, as my father stopped one of the vendors.

"What a *good* girl you are," gushed Clarice. "But I'm going to have candyfloss." So did Dad, to be polite, I suppose. But Jeff and I stuck to popcorn. We weren't ready to go into polite sugar overload for anyone.

Two candyflosses and two popcorns later, we had walked round the entire fairground. My father looked at his watch. "Well, time to go," he said.

"Oh, Schaf, really! I was having such fun," said Clarice.

"Oh, Dad!" said Jeff.

I frowned suspiciously at Jeff. What was he up to now?

Jeff pointed at the Scrambler. "Couldn't we just ride on that?"

"Let's all ride it!" said Clarice, clapping her hands.

I winced. "No thanks," I said. "It's too wild for me."

"Chicken!" said Jeff.

My father said, "I hate to say it but it's probably too much for me, too."

"Oh," said Jeff. "it's no fun alone."

Clarice took the bait. "I'll ride it with

you, Jeff. Schaf, you and Dawn don't mind waiting here, do you?"

"No problem," said my father.

But it *was* a problem. Poor Clarice staggered off the Scrambler and into the nearest toilets and was sick.

"Gosh," said Jeff. "I didn't know she was going to *throw up*."

My father said, "That will be enough, Jeff." Jeff must have realized he was pushing his luck, because he didn't say anything else, not even when Clarice emerged, looking rather pale.

"Are you all right? Is there anything I can do?" my father asked.

"I'll be fine," said Clarice. "Just give me a minute."

Poor Clarice. She must have felt awful. She was quiet all the way to the car and nearly all the way home. I was actually feeling sorry for her—until, as we passed the mall, she sat up and said, "You know, Dawn, we should go shopping together."

"Er, OK," I said.

"And soon," Clarice went on. "For those things that just we girls can shop for."

"Er. . ." I said.

"Schaf, I don't know what you were thinking of, letting Dawn go and buy a bra on her own. It obviously doesn't fit.

You need a woman's touch for that sort of thing."

I was *mortified*.

"Oooh, Dawn," said Jeff. I gave him such a fierce glare that he stopped. "Oh. Sorry," he muttered.

My father said, "Dawn's grown-up enough to handle quite a few things herself. I think this is one of them. . . Here we are."

He pulled the car over to the kerb and got out to walk Clarice to her door. When he came back, I said, "Dad?"

My father started the car and said, "I know, I know." He sighed. "Too bad things didn't work out. She's a nice person but . . ."

This dating business was wearing me out. I didn't see how my father kept it up.

I did mention that he was an eternal optimist, though, didn't I?

Exactly nine days later we were out on another family date.

Barbara Hinkley. My father had met her at the dentist's surgery, which should have been a clue. That and the fact that she turned up for the date—to Cap'n Frank's Fun Fish Fry, where the waiters and waitresses are dressed like buccaneers, the food is served in plastic pirate

71

ships, and the dishes all have sweet little nautical names—wearing a suit.

Don't get me wrong. It was a great looking suit, a pinstripe with a long jacket. She was wearing a beautiful silk wrapover blouse under it, gorgeous gold earrings, and carrying a soft leather clutch bag that matched her high heels.

My father was wearing chinos, an aertex T-shirt, and an anorak. Jeff and I were in nice jeans with cotton jumpers and trainers.

My father seemed disconcerted when she walked through the door of the restaurant (she'd told him she preferred to meet us there) and surveyed the room.

Barbara looked downright disapproving as she walked up to the table and sat down. But all she said was, "What an interesting place, Richard," in a cool, polite voice that said, NOT.

The evening went downhill after that.

"I'll have the Shiver Me Timbers Platter," Jeff said, "with double fries. . ."

"Double fries? That's a fried seafood *platter*, Jeffrey. Surely you're getting enough. You don't want to waste food." Barbara's tone was totally disapproving.

"Dad?" Jeff appealed to our father, who was sitting there looking uncomfortable.

"Jeff can handle it if anybody can, Barbara, believe me," Dad said.

"Double fries," repeated Jeff triumphantly, "And the Whale of a Soft Drink-size coke."

I chose the Schooner Sandwich (with boiled clams) and a green salad (the Sea-Green Delight), which was the healthiest thing I could find on the menu.

Dad chose the Deep Six Claws Platter (crab and lobster).

Barbara said, "I'll have plain boiled fish, lemon on the side, a small green salad, oil and vinegar dressing on the side, and a tonic water with lime."

The waitress, who was wearing a pirate hat said, "The Shoreline Special."

"No," corrected Barbara. "I don't want chips. I don't want coleslaw. I don't want your special sea sauce, whatever that is. *Plain* boiled fish, lemon on the side, a small green salad, oil and vinegar dressing on the side, and a tonic water with lime. And, young lady, I will send it back if it is not as I asked for it."

"Oh!" The waitress's cheeks went pink, but she wrote it all down and said, "Certainly. Anything else?"

That was it. For the entire evening. If you don't count Barbara correcting Jeff and me on our table manners, commenting on what we were eating, trying to prevent Jeff from ordering dessert, urging me to drink some milk because it was especially important for adolescents to get enough calcium, and generally being picky and uptight.

By the time the meal was over, I would have been glad to make her walk the plank. And I was as glad as I've ever been to see her shake my father's hand, say, "Well, it's been an interesting experience," and walk away.

My father stood there for a moment, watching. Then he turned. "Oh, well," he said. "Can't win them all, can you?"

"It's OK, Dad," said Jeff. "The food was great!"

7th
CHAPTER

"So long, Dad!" shouted Whitney cheerfully.

Mr Cater made a face, then smiled. "You sound like you're glad to see me go," he teased gently.

Whitney gave a snort of laughter and threw her arms around her father so hard he rocked backwards. "No," she said, giving him a huge bear hug. "But Dawn's come to see me." She suddenly straightened up and said very formally, "We will see you later."

"OK. 'Bye, Whitney, Dawn."

"Goodbye," said Whitney.

"'Bye, Mr Cater," I said.

We listened as Whitney's father's footsteps crossed the hall. A moment later the front door closed.

"Too bad people have to work," I said,

looking out of Whitney's bedroom window at the bright sunshine. "It's such a great day."

"Great," Whitney echoed.

I looked around the room. Through the half-open door of Whitney's wardrobe. I caught a glimpse of familiar lime-green. It looked like the green panda that Clarice had won for me on the disastrous family date to the fair. I'd given it to Whitney and she had put it proudly on the chair in her room and called it Buster.

"Is that Buster in the wardrobe?" I asked.

Whitney nodded without looking towards Buster.

"Why?"

Her eyebrows closing up in a frown, Whitney said, "Because Buster is for babies. I'm too grown-up for him now."

"Oh." Looking around the room, I realized that all Whitney's dolls and stuffed animals had disappeared—into the wardrobe, I suspected. "I see. Well, so, what do you want to do today?"

Whitney's frown stayed in place. "Something grown-up," she replied. "I want to go to the mall." She sounded as if she expected me to disagree with her. I wondered briefly if it was something that was a special treat for Whitney, or something that her parents didn't do at all. But I couldn't imagine why, nor had they mentioned anything about it.

"Well, we can't go to the big mall because it's too far," I said. Whitney frowned harder. I went on, "But we can walk to the one near here. That'd be great." I watched the frown disappear from Whitney's face as if by magic.

"Great!" she echoed, and made a dive for the piggy bank on her chest of drawers. She emptied it out on her bed, then pulled a large old leather shoulder bag from the top shelf of her wardrobe.

"My mum gave me this," she explained. "It's a grown-up bag, see? It has a zip-up pocket inside and its own matching purse."

Whitney crammed the money from the bed into the purse, then stuck the purse into the zip-up compartment.

"Ready?" I asked.

"Yes," said Whitney excitedly.

"Then let's go."

The mall wasn't far away at all and the walk through Whitney's neighbourhood was a pleasant one. When we reached the big crossroads in front of the mall, I remembered how flustered Whitney had got once before at a crossing, so I linked my arm through hers as we waited for the lights to change. "We're almost there," I said.

Whitney nodded. When we reached the other side, I slipped my arm free of Whitney's and pretended to adjust my rucksack so that Whitney wouldn't think I had been treating her like a baby, leading her across the street.

But Whitney's eyes were focused on Hudson's department store ahead. She kept snapping and unsnapping the clasp on the bag.

"Ready, set, spend!" I joked as we reached the path outside the mall. Whitney just nodded again.

We went to Hudson's. The first things we saw as we walked in the door were the make-up and perfume counters. Whitney made a beeline for them.

She picked up a sample bottle. "Pretty," she said. "What's this?"

I looked at the label. "*Poison*," I read aloud.

Whitney's eyes widened and she put the bottle down quickly.

"No, no, Whitney. It's not really poison. That's the name of the perfume, see?" I picked up the bottle, turned Whitney's wrist over and sprayed a little on it.

Whitney sniffed her wrist, then

wrinkled her nose. I sniffed it, too, and had to agree.

"It's strong," I said. "Phew!"

We walked from counter to counter, smelling the different perfumes.

"Look," said Whitney. She pointed to the Chanel counter. "That's what my mother wears."

"Chanel?" I said. "Very classy." We walked over and I picked up the sample bottle. "Wait a minute, Whitney! You've run out of wrists. You'll have to put some on my wrist."

I was about to hand the bottle to Whitney when a frosty voice said, "May I help you?"

I turned my head and saw a thin woman with frosted hair and a ton of blusher on her cheeks staring at us. Her eyes went from me to Whitney's and widened. She stared at Whitney and I felt a flush of annoyance. She was so rude!

"We're sampling the perfumes," I said in my most grown-up voice.

Without warning, the woman grabbed the bottle from my hand. "Here, I'll do that." She sprayed a tiny amount on my wrist, then said, her voice even colder, "Will there be anything else?"

Whitney looked puzzled.

"No, thank you," I said, making my

voice as frosty as hers. "We've had quite enough of your help. Come on, Whitney."

I turned and stomped away.

"Dawn?"

"Sorry, Whitney. She made me angry. I . . . I suppose she doesn't like her job."

Whitney accepted that. "Can I smell your wrist?" She bent over and sniffed. "My mother's perfume!" she exclaimed in a loud voice. A couple of women standing at a nearby discount make-up table turned and stared. One leaned over and whispered something into the other's ear.

I knew they were talking about Whitney. I glared at them and they saw me and turned away quickly.

Good grief! How could people be so rude? It isn't as if Down's syndrome is all that uncommon. Hadn't people ever seen anyone like Whitney before? Hadn't they ever seen anyone who was a little different?

I had told Whitney how some companies test make-up on animals and hurt them, but I didn't think she'd remembered. However, I realized she had when we next stopped at a make-up counter (where the assistant didn't, for a change, stare at Whitney or act as if she might do something weird). She just smiled and said, "The newest in this line of lipsticks. I'm wearing that colour. Do you girls want to see anything?"

Whitney said, "Do you do things to animals with those?"

The assistant looked surprised for a moment, then said, "Oh, you mean animal testing. No, we don't do animal testing with any of our products, including the perfume."

"Good," said Whitney. With the assistant's help, she tried two of the lipsticks on the back of her hand. "Pretty," she said.

The assistant nodded. "It wears well, too. It will last a long, long time."

I bought some moisturiser with a sunscreen in it and before we left, the assistant reached under the counter and pulled out two tiny bottles attached to cards. "Here's a sample of our perfume for you," she said. "*Oceanambre*. I think you'll like it."

"Thanks!" I said.

Whitney beamed. "Thank you very much," she said in her best grown-up voice.

People weren't so bad, after all, I was deciding as we walked out of the shop. I lifted my face to the sun coming through the skylights above and was feeling pretty good as we walked under the potted palms. But it was too soon to relax, as I quickly discovered.

At least half the people we passed stared at Whitney. A lot of them whispered to one another or giggled or both. It was disgusting.

"Look!" cried Whitney.

People turned, people stared, people giggled and whispered. How could Whitney not notice? Didn't it hurt her?

But she didn't seem to associate the reactions of those around her with herself. She pointed at the hair-bead shop and practically dragged me in.

Now it was Whitney's turn to stare. The manageress had dozens and dozens of beaded braids of hair all over her head. They made a clicking sound when she moved. It was really spectacular.

"Ohhh!" breathed Whitney. She pointed. "I want my hair to look like that."

"Don't point, Whitney. It's rude," I whispered automatically, as if she were one of my regular babysitting charges. Oops!

But she lowered her arm obediently and the manageress smiled.

"It took me a long time to get my hair this way, dear," she said. "And you need good strong hair to do it. Yours might be a little too thin for that. But come on over here and let's see what we can do."

After much deliberation, Whitney chose a set of beads and the manageress wove them into a strand of her hair. Whitney examined herself in the mirror and said, "It's beautiful. Isn't it beautiful, Dawn?"

"Yes it is, Whitney," I said.

The manageress nodded. "They'll all slip off if you undo the bottom part of the strand, here," she explained. "But you can keep them in while you wash your hair if you want. Some beads you can't, of course, but these you can."

Opening her purse, Whitney carefully counted out her money.

"Thank you," she said as we left.

"My pleasure," said the manageress. "Come back soon."

From the bead shop, Whitney zoomed into the earring shop. She immediately wanted to get her ears pierced.

"No," I said flatly.

"Why not? You've got yours pierced, Dawn. I want my ears to be pierced, too."

"Whitney, I had to get my parents' permission to do this. I tell you what. If your parents agree that you can get your ears pierced, we'll come back and do it, OK?"

Whitney sighed, but she said, "OK."

"Meanwhile, what about some stick-on earrings?" I asked.

Bending forward, Whitney peered at the sheet of stick-on earrings to which I was pointing.

Suddenly the woman beside us turned. She stared at Whitney, then jerked away so quickly she bumped into the counter behind her. Then she began to back away, still staring.

Staring at Whitney. Acting as if Whitney had some kind of contagious disease, or was dirty or something.

Next to me, Whitney said, "I want these," and opened her purse. She never seemed to notice.

When she had bought the earrings, Whitney stuck a pair of red flowers on her earlobes. Then we went to try on hats with her new look: big hats, silly hats, baseball caps. It was a lot of fun.

Or it would have been, if I hadn't been so aware now of how awful people were acting. At last I couldn't take it any more. I had had enough.

I took off a big straw hat with a giant flower and put it back on the hat stand. "Time to go, Whitney," I said, trying to make my voice cheerful and unconcerned.

"Really?" Reluctantly, Whitney took

off a sequined baseball cap and put it back.

We walked out into the mall and made our way towards the exit. At the last minute, Whitney veered away.

"Whitney," I began.

"Just one more shop, Dawn, OK? Please?"

"Well. . ."

"Please, please, please?"

I couldn't help but smile. "OK."

Whitney grabbed my arm. "By myself. I want to do this by myself."

Seeing the objection in my face, she hurried on, "I'll just go right there. You can wait here for me." She pointed at a shop that had a neon "Wild Things" sign above the entrance. Through the glass I could see stacks of multicoloured socks, shelves of trolls, and all sorts of bits and pieces.

"OK," I said.

Whitney thrust the bag holding the sheet of earrings into my hands then hurried off, her arms swinging and the bag swinging by her side. She looked happy and excited.

At least to me. I wondered what she looked like to all the rude people who whispered and stared as she rushed by.

A few minutes later, Whitney emerged

clutching a shopping bag. "Here," she said.

I opened the bag and Whitney reached inside and pulled out a Best Friends necklace. Carefully, ceremoniously, she gave me half.

"Because you are my best friend," Whitney said, looking intently at me, her cheeks pink. "My best friend in the whole world."

I looked down at the necklace, then back at Whitney.

Whitney had started out as a job. But she had become a friend, too.

"Oh, Whitney, thank you," I said softly. "I'll keep this for ever."

And I knew that I would.

8th CHAPTER

"Dawn, Jeff, I'm glad to meet you."

Karina Whitaker held out her hand and shook our hands.

"Hey!" said Jeff, and I could tell he was impressed.

"I'm glad to meet you, too," I said, and this time I thought that maybe I meant it.

We were about to go out on another one of our family dates with our father. But Karina actually seemed nice and normal: not too formal, not too loud, not too anything else.

"Well, then, let's go," said my father, looking pleased. "The wonderful world of performances *al fresco* waits for no man. Or woman."

Performances *al fresco* meant performances outside. We were going to an outdoor concert, classical music but cool-sounding classical music, with lots of special effects and great-looking musicians. At least, I thought they were great-looking when we got there.

I thought the crowd looked pretty cool, too. Lots of families with their babysitting charges, er, I mean their children, and an incredible variety of picnic baskets and chairs and rugs and food smells. We got there early to find a good seat and we did, close enough to watch the band (or maybe I mean orchestra) set up, but far enough away so we weren't right in the middle of a million people.

Of course, Jeff spotted somebody he knew immediately and zoomed off after swiping a muesli bar out of the basket. Dad and Karina and I laughed and began to spread out the rug and the picnic.

It was a pretty great picnic, if I do say so myself. I'd helped Mrs B prepare it, and I enjoyed listening to Karina and my father ooh and ah as I took out tiny cherry tomatoes stuffed with spicy cheese filling; avocado, spinach, and red onion sandwiches with walnut oil vinaigrette on granary bread; mozzarella sandwiches with roasted red peppers and pickled mushrooms on Italian bread; peanut butter and apple sandwiches on wholewheat bread; new potato salad with dill; and grapes and strawberries and kiwi fruit salad with poppy seed dressing. As well as muesli bars for snacks.

"And for dessert we have cheesecake with raspberry sauce," I announced, taking the last bottle of sparkling water out of the cooler.

"This is *amazing*, Dawn" said Karina. "You must have worked for *hours*."

"Healthy and delicious-looking," said my father. "Thank you, Dawn."

"Any time," I said airily, but I was pleased. Then I saw Sunny and her family nearby. Sunny hadn't seen us yet, so I jumped up. "I'm going to go and say hello to Sunny," I told Dad. "I'll be right back."

Sunny didn't see me till I was right behind her and tapped her on the shoulder. She turned and I realized she was wearing her radio headphones.

"Dawn!" she cried in a voice that you could hear all the way to the ocean.

I winced and put my hands over my ears and pointed to the headphones.

Sunny reached up, took them off, and grinned. "Sorry," she said in a normal tone of voice.

"This is supposed to be a concert," I said.

"Yes, but what if I don't like the

music?" Sunny asked. "A good babysitter is always prepared."

"True," I said. "But I think this is going to be kind of cool. Look, there are the Austins."

We turned and waved at the girls, then watched the crowd. The slope in front of the park bandshell was filling up fast.

"Look at that," said Sunny. "Someone's brought a whole sound system practically. You'd think they could go without music till the concert started!"

"Very prepared," I said. "Or something!"

We watched people and gossiped till the musicians finished tuning up. Then I went back to Dad and Karina. Jeff joined us a minute later and we sat down and began to load our plates.

I speared a tomato and gave the sky (still blue, but turning dark with a few stars appearing) an approving glance, and a figure plonked down on the rug next to me.

"Dawn!" said Whitney happily. "You're wearing your friendship necklace, just like me."

"Whitney, hey! Of course I am," I said softly. "I didn't see you."

"We've just got here," said Whitney. She turned and pointed behind her and I saw the Caters sitting a little way away. I waved and they waved back and Mrs Cater, who'd been leaning slightly forward, leaned back and seemed to relax.

"What're you eating? It looks good," said Whitney.

"Didn't you bring a picnic?"

Whitney shook her head regretfully. "We had dinner at home."

"Here," I said, and made Whitney a sort of sampler plate with just a little of everything.

"Karina, could you hand me the salt?" I asked, pouring Whitney some soda water.

Karina didn't answer. "Karina?" I handed Whitney the soda and looked over at Karina.

Karina was looking at Whitney. With a sinking heart, I saw that the expression on her face was a familiar one: repulsion. And embarrassment.

Hoping I was wrong (after all, it was getting dark), I tried again. "Karina? The salt?"

Karina looked away.

I reached over and got the salt myself.

"MMMMM, this is good, Dawn," said Whitney.

"Cherry tomatoes with spicy cheese

filling," I said. "It's sort of a variation on a recipe I had in this great vegetarian restaurant once."

"A vegetable restaurant?" asked Whitney.

Next to me, Jeff nodded. "That's exactly what it is," he said. "No hot dogs. No hamburgers."

I laughed. "Not exactly," I said. "But it's true they don't serve meat."

"Well, you could open a vegetarian restaurant any time with this meal," said Dad.

Karina remained rigidly silent next to him, her eyes down on her plate, picking at her food.

One of the musicians leaned forward and grabbed the mike. It made that horrible microphone sound and then he said, "Your attention, please, ladies and gentlemen. . ."

"Perfect timing," said my father. "Dessert is cheesecake *and* music."

"Cheesecake. I love cheesecake," said Whitney happily.

Karina, not quite looking at Whitney, said, "I think it's time you went back and joined your parents."

"That's OK," said Whitney. "They said I could stay if it was all right with Dawn."

92

"Great," I said firmly. "I think you'll like the cheesecake."

I cut some cheesecake for Whitney, Dad, Jeff and me. But not for Karina, because when I got to her she said, "I couldn't possibly."

"I've eaten a lot, too," said Dad. "Wait a little while. You'll have room. We'll save you a piece, won't we, Sunshine?"

Poor Dad. I could tell he'd noticed Karina's behaviour, too. Now he was all nervous and jolly, trying to make things OK.

Karina's next remark didn't help. "It's not that I'm full. It's just that the scenery has made me lose my appetite."

My father frowned. My mouth dropped open. Jeff, of course, kept on eating. And luckily, Whitney didn't seem to hear. Or if she did, she didn't understand.

"This is good, Dawn," she said.

"I'm glad you like it," I managed to answer. "Listen, the music is about to begin."

I'd been right about thinking the music would be cool. It was. The musicians explained a little about each piece, played some variations on the opening bars of each one so we could see what it might have sounded like at the time it was writ-ten, then launched into their own cool, funky versions of the classical pieces by guys like Bach and Mozart.

"I like this," said Whitney next to me. As the band launched into another piece, she stood up and began to try to dance, throwing her hands out and making up a song to go with the music. She sang loudly. Of course people turned to look, but Whitney kept on dancing and singing happily, not seeming to notice.

OK, it wasn't the most appropriate thing to do at a concert. But it wasn't as if it were a formal performance in Carnegie Hall or something, either. And at least Whitney was really enjoying the music, not just nodding off like some of the people around me. I reached up and caught Whitney's arm and said, "That sounds good, Whitney, but I think some people want to listen to the music without the words."

"Oh, OK," said Whitney cheerfully. She sat back down and turned her face towards the stage, and watched and listened intently all the way through to the end of the piece.

Then Karina said, softly but clearly, "That was disgusting."

Had Whitney heard? No. I gave Karina the meanest look I could, then grabbed Whitney's hand, stood up, and pulled her to her feet. "Come on, let's go back to your parents."

We walked over to them and Whitney said, "Dawn had a picnic. I had a picnic, too."

"Not too much," I said. "A sample picnic. Whitney said you'd had dinner already."

Mrs Cater smiled and said, "Great. Come on Whitney, sit here by me." Whitney sat down and I said, "Do you mind if I join you for a while?"

"Not at all," said Mr Cater. The Caters made room for me on their rug and I stayed with them for the rest of the concert. I knew it was rude of me not to join Dad and Jeff and Karina, but I didn't care.

I didn't care if I never saw Karina again. I couldn't believe how rude and insensitive and totally obnoxious she had been about Whitney.

What a big loser Karina was. Mentally, I drew a big, black X through her name on Dad's date list.

9th CHAPTER

Saturday

What is that saying?
All is fair in love and war?
Well, love and war have
broken out at the Barretts.
Mrs. Barrett and Mr. DeWitt
are getting married, and
that means two happy
adults and seven very
cranky kids. I tried to
tell them about my
combined family, and
yours, Kristy, but they
weren't interested.

Mary Anne had a two-part job on Saturday afternoon: stay with the three Barretts while Mrs Barrett ran errands, then stay with Mrs Barrett and help her get dinner ready for Franklin and his four children. It was an unusual job, but when she described it to me later, we realized it went beyond unusual.

Mrs Barrett opened the door the moment Mary Anne knocked. She was beaming and without saying a word she held out her left hand. A beautiful ring sparkled on her third finger.

"Oh!" gasped Mary Anne. "An engagement ring!"

Mrs Barrett nodded and stepped back. "Yes. The night of that cocktail party. He asked me then. It was so wonderful."

Mary Anne remembered that was the night that Claudia and Stacey had been sitting for the seven kids, and she remembered how happy the two adults had been acting. So that's what it was! Love and a marriage proposal.

"Ooh, this is *so* exciting!" cried Mary Anne. She was really thrilled. A proposal meant a wedding, and to Mary Anne, the world's most romantic and sensitive person, a wedding is a world-class event. Mary Anne threw her arms around Mrs Barrett and gave her a big hug.

Then she began to fire a million questions at Mrs Barrett, like when was the wedding, and where, and where would they live, and would there be bridesmaids, and what was Mrs Barrett going to wear.

"Whoa!" said Mrs Barrett, laughing. "The wedding is in December. Let's see—we'll all be moving into one house. I'll take DeWitt for my new surname, but Buddy, Suzi and Marnie will stay Barretts, of course. Buddy will be the ringbearer and Lindsey will be the flowergirl. I don't know what I'm wearing yet. Or what flowers I'll carry," she added, anticipating Mary Anne's next question.

Mary Anne nodded but her mind was already racing ahead. "The BSC will help in any way it can," she promised (meaning that she especially would be glad to help with a wedding).

Mrs Barrett looked pleased. "Why, thank you, Mary Anne. That's very sweet of you."

"This is so, so, so great," said Mary Anne, clasping her hands together.

"I think so, too," Mrs Barrett said, looking suddenly shy and actually blushing a little. Then she looked at her watch, shook her wrist, held her watch to her ear and cried, "It's accurate. Oh, I'm *late*!"

Mrs Barrett practically flew out of the

door and it wasn't till Mary Anne had waved goodbye that she realized that in all her excitement over the forthcoming wedding possibilities, she hadn't seen a single Barrett kid. She knew Marnie was having a nap, but where were Buddy and Suzi? At least one of them usually met her at the door when she arrived.

"Buddy?" she called (not too loudly, so she wouldn't wake up Marnie). "Suzi?"

No one answered, but she could hear the sound of the television from the playroom.

Sure enough, Buddy and Suzi were sitting on the sofa in front of the television.

"Hey," said Mary Anne, walking in. "What is this? Celebrity Mud Wrestling? I don't believe it!"

Buddy just kept staring straight ahead at the TV, his arms folded and his lower lip sticking out. So did Suzi.

"You two, are you telling me you find mud wrestling more interesting than me? That hurts!"

Suzi flashed Mary Anne a look out of the corner of her eyes. "You're glad she's getting married!" she said. "We heard you!"

Well, *that* caught Mary Anne off guard. She'd been so taken up with the whole wedding scenario that she'd forgotten that

Buddy and Suzi might not feel the same way.

"Oh. Yes, I *am* glad for your mother. She seems very happy," Mary Anne answered carefully.

"Well, we're not!" Buddy burst out. "I hate all those DeWitts."

"Me, too!" echoed Suzi.

"And I don't want any more brothers and sisters, either."

"Me, too." That was Suzi again.

"Wow!" said Mary Anne softly, looking at the two agitated and *very* cross children in front of her. She pointed at the TV. "Do you mind if I turn this off?"

"OK," said Buddy grudgingly.

Mary Anne turned off the television, then turned to face the Barretts.

"You know, my father got married again," she began. "And I got a new family when he did. Now I've got a new sister who is also one of my best friends and—"

She didn't get to finish.

"No!" said Buddy. "NO! NO! NO!"

"I don't want to share my room with them," cried Suzi. "I like my room. It's *my* room."

"It's not so bad sharing. . ." Mary Anne tried again.

"And it's our house," said Buddy. "We

don't need them in our house." He bounced up off the sofa and looked around. "I know. I know what we can do."

"What?" Suzi bounced up, too.

"We can DeWitt-proof the house. Like in that old film, *Swiss Family Robinson*, when they build all those traps for the pirates, remember?"

Mary Anne tried to look stern, but inside she was stifling a sympathetic laugh. The DeWitts as pirates? Good grief!

"Yes!" Suzi nodded emphatically. "DeWitt traps!"

With that, Buddy was off.

Rather than try to talk Buddy and Suzi out of their project, Mary Anne decided to let them work some steam out of their systems for a while, tagging along to keep an eye on things to make sure they didn't get out of hand. And maybe she could gradually make Buddy and Suzi see reason while she was at it. Then Mrs Barrett could talk to them when she got home and help Buddy and Suzi de-DeWitt-proof the house before the dinner party.

Buddy and Suzi's first project was DeWitt-proofing their rooms. While Mary Anne watched, the two kids filled saucepans with water and put them just inside the door, tied strings to the door handles, and attached them to the backs of chairs so that the chairs would tip over when the doors were opened. Then they made big signs that said, "DeWitts keep out, or else!"

"There," said Buddy, helping Suzi tape the last corner of her sign on her door. "That should do it."

"It looks effective," said Mary Anne truthfully.

Buddy looked around, then said, "Ha!" A moment later he was carefully rubbing vaseline on the doorknob of the bathroom he and Suzi shared. "See, I'm leaving this part at the back without vaseline," he explained to Suzi. "so we can open it, 'cause we know the secret."

Suzi nodded and helped Buddy make a sign that said, "Barrett bathroom *only*."

Next came the playroom. Buddy and Suzi made signs and put them on the chairs and sofa: Buddy's, Suzi's, Marnie's.

"You know," Mary Anne tried again, "Kristy's family is a combined family and it's great. They have a lot of fun. There are as many as *ten* people in Kristy's house sometimes, not counting their pets. It's always interesting. Something amazing is always happening."

It was like talking to a wall. Buddy said, "I suppose we can't put signs on all the chairs. We'll have to do something else to the other chairs."

"I know!" cried Suzi. She charged off and came back a minute later with towels and a big container of baby talcum powder. Spreading the white towels across the seats of the unlabelled chairs, she dusted them liberally with powder.

"When they sit down, it'll make a big puff!" she said happily.

"Excellent!" said Buddy.

The rest of the afternoon went like that. The Barretts went from room to room, labelling things, making DeWitt traps (although Mary Anne stopped them from doing things like putting buckets of water on the edges of partly opened doors) and ignoring any positive thing Mary Anne might have to say about her combined family or Kristy's, or about how much fun weddings might be.

At last she gave up, got Marnie up from her nap, and changed her clothes (and kept the kids from labelling Marnie as Barrett property). By the time they sat down to a snack of fruit and milk just before Mrs Barrett was due back, the house was thoroughly DeWitt-proofed, and Mary Anne was contemplating spending at least part of the time scheduled for helping Mrs Barrett with dinner before the DeWitts came over, taking down traps and removing signs.

Wrong.

To Mary Anne's horror, it wasn't just Mrs Barrett who came through the door. It was Mrs Barrett and Franklin and all four DeWitt children.

"No!" gasped Mary Anne, rising to her feet. In her usual Mrs Barrett way, she'd changed plans on the spur of the moment.

"We can *all* cook dinner together!" Mrs Barrett announced cheerfully.

"Huh!" said Buddy.

Mary Anne managed to head them off for a moment by persuading the DeWitt kids to sit down for a snack (Buddy and Suzi immediately got up and went back to the playroom). But she wasn't able to catch Mrs Barrett's eye and warn her, so Mary Anne flew through the house, snatching down signs and deactivating "traps".

But she wasn't fast enough. Suddenly she heard a shriek from the playroom. She raced in to see Lindsey sitting on one of the towel-covered chairs, a cloud of white powder floating in the air around her and powder all over her face and hair.

Buddy and Suzi burst out laughing.

Then Taylor, who'd come in behind Mary Anne, saw the signs on the chairs. "What does that mean?" Taylor asked, pointing.

"That DeWitts aren't welcome in *our* house. Or *our* family. We don't need you. So there!" said Buddy.

"Buddy!" said Mary Anne.

Another cry sounded in the hall and Madeleine came in crying "Ugh! Ugh! Ugh!" and holding out her hands. Lindsey looked at Madeleine's hands and said, "Gross! She's got slimy stuff all over her hands."

"The sign said that bathroom was for Barretts only. That'll teach you to use our things without permission!" declared Suzi.

"Fine!" said Lindsey. "We don't want anything to do with your stupid things or your stupid family, anyway. You can go and fry your head in peanut butter."

The DeWitts marched out, leaving Buddy and Suzi looking angry but triumphant.

Miraculously, Mrs Barrett and Franklin didn't seem to have noticed anything amiss yet. They were in the kitchen beginning preparations for dinner. Mary Anne helped, and, every chance she got, dashed out to move another sign or take apart another booby trap. But by the time she got ready to go, she hadn't succeeded in finding them all.

She left Franklin and Mrs Barrett in the kitchen, talking and laughing as they chopped vegetables for beef stew, while the Barretts sat in the playroom with the DeWitts, playing a silent, deadly game of Monopoly in the living room.

"Mine, mine, mine!" she heard Taylor say as she walked out of the door.

"You know, I don't think Buddy and Suzi are too happy with the idea of sharing their family with the DeWitts," Mary Anne said to Mrs Barrett as she left.

"That's all right, dear," said Mrs Barrett. "They like the DeWitts."

Mary Anne sighed. She'd tried. There was nothing she could do.

But she sensed a disastrous evening ahead for the Barretts and the DeWitts.

10th
CHAPTER

"Here," I said. I handed Whitney the sun-block and leaned back with a sigh. Another perfect California day, and Whitney and I were celebrating by spending the whole afternoon outdoors in the shade of a tree.

Of course, it's hard to get sunburned sitting under a tree, but I knew how easily Whitney burned and I wasn't taking any chances. Whitney reminded me a little of the time Kristy's little sister Karen had decided to become grown-up all at once by copying everything she saw Kristy and the other members of the BSC do. If Whitney saw me putting on sunblock, she put it on, too, without a question.

I pushed my sunglasses up on my nose and sighed a sigh of perfect contentment. Whitney pushed her glasses up, then frowned. "Are you unhappy, Dawn?"

Realizing that Whitney was talking about my sigh, I smiled and said quickly, 'No way. That was a sigh of happiness.''

Whitney smiled then, too. "Good," she said.

We sat in silence for a little while, soaking up the soft warmth of the air and the outdoors-in-the-neighbourhood noises all around us: someone washing a car (not as energy efficient as a car wash, but just this once I'd overlook it), birds, the distant sound of a dog barking, the rhythmic *snap-snap-snap* of hand shears from someone trimming a hedge (the old-fashioned way, without electricity).

Then Whitney said, "I'm hungry."

"Mmm," I said. "Not now, Whitney."

"I want another ice-cream sandwich."

"You had one just after your mother left this afternoon. Why don't you wait till your parents get home and have another one after dinner?" I asked. What I didn't want to say was that Whitney simply couldn't have another ice-cream sandwich. The last thing Mrs Cater had said to me before she left earlier was, "We're going out to dinner this evening, so don't let Whitney eat anything after three o'clock. I don't want her to spoil her appetite."

In a normal babysitting situation, I could have said, "I'm sorry, you can't have another ice-cream sandwich, Whitney. Your parents said so, and I'm responsible for seeing to it that you do what they say. That's the rule."

"I don't want to wait till after dinner," Whitney answered. Then she added coaxingly, "Aren't you hungry, too, Dawn?"

I laughed and shook my head. "I haven't got your sweet tooth, Whitney."

That distracted Whitney for a minute. "What's a sweet tooth?"

"Oh. It's, well, it's just a way of saying that you like sweet things a lot."

"I do," agreed Whitney, nodding again. She reached up and tapped her finger against one of her front teeth and laughed loudly.

Then she jumped to her feet and went to the back door.

"Whitney? Whitney!" I called. I jumped to my feet and ran after her.

She was opening the freezer door when I caught up with her.

"Whitney, no. You can't have another ice-cream sandwich." I put my hand on the freezer door and closed it firmly.

Just as firmly, Whitney kept her fingers wrapped around the door handle. "I *want* another ice-cream sandwich," she said stubbornly.

"Just wait a little while, OK?" I said.

Whitney sighed.

Taking that as acceptance of my words, I took my hand off the door.

Quickly Whitney yanked the door open and grabbed the box of ice-cream sandwiches.

Even more quickly, I grabbed the box from Whitney's hands. "No!" I said, more sharply than I had intended. I shoved the box back in the freezer, closed the door, and turned to face an infuriated Whitney.

"I *can* have another sandwich! I can have as many as I want. You're not my boss!" cried Whitney.

"Whitney, I'm your babysitter and I—" I stopped in horror, clapping my hand over my mouth.

But it was too late.

Whitney's eyes widened. Her expression grew stricken. "You're my *babysitter*?" she repeated incredulously.

"Er, well, it's not exactly that," I began lamely. What could I say? I could lie, try to pretend it was a big joke.

But I knew that Whitney would know. She'd know I was lying and that would hurt her feelings even more.

110

"Dawn?" asked Whitney.

"I—" I looked into Whitney's eyes. I knew she knew.

"Yes, I'm your babysitter. Your parents hired me to stay with you in the afternoons till your camp starts. They didn't want you to be alone."

The stricken look left Whitney's face, to be replaced by one of humiliation. And anger. And betrayal.

"Oh, Whitney. It's not what you think. I mean, I. . ."

"I thought you were my friend!" Whitney yelled. "I thought you were my *friend*!"

The last word ended on a long, drawn-out wail as Whitney turned and stomped out of the room.

"Whitney, wait! I *am* your friend. Whitney?"

The sound of a door slamming and being locked was my only answer.

Whitney spent the rest of the afternoon in her room and nothing I said or did could get her to come out or even to answer me.

When her mother got back, I talked to Mrs Cater for a little while. She wasn't too upset. She just shook her head and said, "Maybe it wasn't the best way to go about it, after all. But it's not your fault,

111

Dawn. Just give her time." I went to say goodbye to Whitney through the door. It opened then, and for a moment I hoped Whitney had forgiven me.

I was wrong. Her face wooden, her eyes accusing, Whitney said, "Give me back the necklace."

"The Best Friends necklace? Whitney, you don't mean that, do you?"

Wrong question.

"I do!" Whitney yelled, her eyes filling with tears. "I mean it for ever."

And when I'd given her back the necklace, she slammed the door again and locked me out once more.

I thought of Whitney all that night. I felt terrible: terrible about the lie, terrible about how badly I had handled the whole thing.

I tried to imagine how Whitney must feel. As an imaginary feeling, it was pretty awful. For Whitney it must have been a hundred times worse.

The next morning, I rang Mrs Cater as early as I could.

"How's Whitney?" I asked.

"She stayed in her room all night," Mrs Cater told me. Her voice sounded sad and tired. "I'm so sorry that this happened."

"If only I'd been more careful," I said.

"No. No, we should have told Whitney

right from the start. But she works so hard at being 'grown-up' and self-reliant and we wanted to give her support in that. We were afraid saying you were her babysitter would undermine that positive self-image." Mrs Cater paused, then went on in a tone of forced cheerfulness, "Still, Whitney's always so sweet and good-natured. She'll get over it. I'm sure of that."

"Should I come this afternoon?"

"Yes. Yes, you need to be here. And maybe that will help," Mrs Cater told me.

So I went to the Caters' that afternoon as usual.

"Whitney's in her room," said Mrs Cater, who met me at the door.

"Is she. . ."

Mrs Cater nodded. "But the door's open. That's a good sign, I think."

I certainly hoped so. As soon as Mrs Cater had gone, I went to Whitney's room.

Whitney was sitting on the floor, looking at a magazine.

"Hi, Whitney!" I said.

No answer.

"Is that a good magazine? I don't think I've seen that one yet."

I might as well have been talking to myself.

Although I kept trying, Whitney didn't speak to me the whole afternoon.

Or the next.

Then on the third afternoon, she looked up from the puzzle she was doing and said, "I'm not a baby. I don't need a baby-sitter."

Taking this as an opening, I said, "You're not a baby. That's true. Baby-sitter isn't the word I should have used."

Whitney turned her back on me.

She didn't speak to me again until I saw her go by with a basketful of laundry.

"What's happening?" I said.

Whitney kept walking towards the laundry room. I followed her. I watched as she sorted out the clothes and began to put them into the washing machine.

"Want some help?" I asked.

"I'm not a baby," said Whitney. "I can do it myself."

After that, no matter what happened, Whitney seemed determined to prove that she didn't need any help at all with anything, determined to prove that she was grown-up and didn't need me at all.

After a dozen attempts to join Whitney in whatever she was doing or to coax her into joining me, and being told, "I'm not a baby. I don't need a babysitter," I gave up.

114

At least on that approach.

I had hurt Whitney and there was nothing I could do to change that. All I could do now was wait and hope she could work things out for herself.

And then maybe she would forgive me.

11th CHAPTER

"Take me out to the old ball game," my father sang, loudly and off-key.

I winced.

Jeff said, "*Dad!*"

Dad stopped singing and pulled his jacket on. "Kayla's job with the public relations firm is not only challenging, but it has special perks. The tickets she got for us this evening are for the best seats."

Those words brought out the more tolerant side of Jeff. "Cool!" he said.

I didn't say anything. I like baseball, don't get me wrong. But I wasn't sure I liked the idea of spending a whole evening at a California Angels game all the way over in Anaheim.

"What's Kayla like?" I asked as I followed Dad and Jeff to the car.

"She's in public relations," my father told me. Again.

"And she likes baseball?" I said.

"Looks like it," my father agreed. He concentrated on backing out of the drive, then said casually, over his shoulder, "By the way, Kayla's daughter will be joining us. Kayla loved the idea of a family date and wanted Alana to come, too."

Alana. That was an unusual name. I'd only met one other person with that name, a classmate who was a bit of a pain. No, wrong, who was a *big* pain.

But it probably wasn't the same Alana, I told myself. Couldn't be. It was one thing to believe in ghosts, another to believe in wild coincidences.

Maybe Alana wasn't such an unusual name after all. Maybe it was one of those popular names for a new generation. Maybe I just hadn't heard about the new name-your-kid-Alana trend. I fervently hoped so.

Wrong. Alana was *the* Alana. Alana the Pain from my school.

I could tell she was just as thrilled to see me.

Kayla slid into the car next to our father and turned to smile at us. She had a nice smile. She and Alana sort of looked alike, too.

But if Alana had a smile like her mother's, we weren't going to find out about it that night.

Alana opened the car door, looked in, and said in a completely flat voice, "It *is* you."

Any thought I'd had of welcoming her died right there. I folded my arms and turned to stare out the window.

It was so totally weird. It wasn't as if Alana and I were total enemies. We weren't. We didn't even know each other that well.

But we hung out in completely different crowds. Alana's crowd could have been labelled "Brains Trust," or "Rocket Scientists of the Future". She and her friends always got top marks, were always winning merit awards and honourable mentions and doing extra work for extra credit. They sat together at the same table in the canteen and talked more quietly and seriously than everybody else. But if you listened to their conversations, they didn't sound like conversations at all. The words were big and the concepts were complicated, but it seemed more as if they were showing off how much they knew than enjoying knowing it.

Not like me and my friends: study hard, work hard (and be great babysitters), play hard, and don't forget to surf. That could have been our motto. Needless to say, we made more noise at our lunch table.

And I didn't have to be a future rocket scientist to know that Alana and her crowd looked down on us for being the way we were.

I wasn't happy with this set-up. I didn't think Alana was, either.

But I did try, at least a little. After a few minutes, I cleared my throat and said, in Alana's general direction, "So, do you like baseball?"

"It's a silly game," said Alana.

I frowned. She was calling my father and Jeff—and her mother—silly. And me, too, for that matter, even if I wasn't as big a baseball fan as my brother and father.

Still, I decided to try to be polite. "I can see how people might not like baseball," I said. "What sports do you like?"

Alana looked over at me and raised one eyebrow. Her expression was disdainful. "Sports don't interest me," she said.

"Oh," I said.

I could take a hint.

I leaned forward and said to Kayla, "Do you like sport?"

Kayla smiled at me and nodded. "You're not going to believe this, but I used to be on my fencing team in college."

"There's a sport for you, Dawn," said Alana sarcastically.

Her mother ignored her and went on, "These days, I make do with tennis."

"Fencing?" I said, impressed. "Was it hard?"

"Wow! What an incisive question," muttered Alana.

I bared my teeth in what wasn't a smile and turned to Alana. "What did you say, Alana?"

Everyone was quiet. Then Alana said. "Nothing." She turned to look out of the window.

Dad cleared his throat. "Here we are," he said.

At the stadium, Dad and Kayla had plenty to say about where to park the car. I was beginning to see where Alana got her way of speaking. Kayla had the same sort of sarcastic way of saying things. It bothered me, but I thought my Dad could handle it. For that matter, I knew Alana was just one of the Brains Trust snobs and I could handle that. I just hated to waste a whole evening on it.

At last Dad and Kayla compromised on a parking spot, and we were on our way into the game.

If you've ever been to a baseball game, you know that the roar of the crowd and the smell of hot dogs are two big, big factors. The roar of the crowd I can take, but not the hot dogs. So when Dad bought hot dogs with mustard for Alana, Kayla, Jeff and himself (although I knew he and Jeff weren't big hot dog fans), I was prepared. I opened my rucksack and brought out an avocado and bean sprout sandwich, a wholewheat blueberry muffin, and an orange.

"What *is* that green stuff?" Alana's voice cut into my satisfied contemplation of my healthy baseball game food.

"Avocado spread," I said. "Do you want to try some?"

"You've *got* to be kidding," said Alana. "I can't believe anyone would be so weird as to bring health food to a baseball game."

Then she took a big bite of hot dog.

I couldn't help it. I made a disgusting gagging sound.

Alana looked pained and swallowed quickly. Then she turned her back on me.

"You girls doing all right?" my father asked.

"Fine, Jack," said Alana.

Jack? Since when did Alana call my father Jack?

But Dad didn't seem to notice. He nodded and turned his attention back to

121

the stadium. A moment later, he was leaping to his feet, trying to get a wave started, cheering loudly.

Under her breath, Alana muttered, "Jerk!"

"What did you say?" I heard my voice go up.

Alana gave me a small superior smile. "Shh! You don't want to upset Jack the jerk, do you?"

I couldn't believe my ears. "What?" I repeated, leaning forward.

Alana opened her mouth. And shrieked as I dumped my lemon and lime drink on to her lap.

"You did that on purpose!" she spluttered, scrubbing at the wet spot with her paper napkin.

"Alana the genius," I retorted, giving her a mean smile.

The game went on for ever. Alana and I ignored one another for nine long innings. Dad spent the time shouting things like "Good play!" while Kayla said things like, "You call that a good play, Jack? Really? How . . . interesting."

When we'd dropped Alana and Kayla off, no one needed to say it aloud: the family date had been a big failure.

Jeff and I settled down for the Saturday midnight monster movie. Dad, looking discouraged, said, "I'm going to call it a night. See you two tomorrow."

After he'd left, Jeff said, "Yuck!"

"Double yuck!" I said. "Where does Dad find these people?"

"The supermarket," Jeff answered. "The video shop. Work."

"Yeah, and Monsters R Us," I added. I paused then went on, "Remember Carol?"

"Yeah," said Jeff.

We were both silent for a moment, thinking about Carol. She and Dad had actually been engaged. But then they'd decided they weren't compatible and called it off.

Jeff and I hadn't been all that keen on Dad remarrying and we hadn't given Carol much of a chance. I wondered now if maybe we hadn't been wrong. All Carol had ever done was try too hard to be nice—something any normal person might do, especially if she loved someone and wanted his family to like her.

Normal. All these people we'd had family dates with had been "normal". Nice, normal people who were nasty to people who were different from them, or full of weird rules and regulations, or just plain obnoxious.

I was sick of normal people. Dad

123

deserved someone better than that. Someone like Carol.

I looked at Jeff. He looked at me. I knew we were thinking the same thing.

"We've got to get Carol and Dad back together," I said aloud.

Jeff put up his hand, and we gave each other the high-five.

12th CHAPTER

Saturday

Well, we've been house hunting.

Yes, It's important to have a big house when you have a big family.

You're the expert, Kristy! After all, you not only have a big family, you have a ghost relative who has his own room!

True, Shannon. Good thing I didn't mention that to the Barrett and the DeWitt kids, though. They might have used that as one of their requirements for picking out a new house: resident ghost required.

It's not too much to ask, is it? After all, when Dawn and Mary Anne's family got together, they got to live in a haunted house.

Also true. Wait'll we write to Dawn about all this...

125

In spite of the war between the Barretts and the DeWitts, the wedding between Mrs Barrett and Mr DeWitt was still on. Kristy had been hearing some of the details of the wedding, since her mum and Mrs Barrett were friends. Of course Kristy, being Kristy, hadn't paid much attention to important details like who was wearing what and what the flowers were going to be. But she did remember to tell the BSC that the Barretts and the DeWitts were *not* going to live together in one or the other of the two families' houses. Instead, they were going to buy a new, bigger house for the whole family. They'd never planned that one of the families would share the other's house, because they knew that it would be a tight squeeze and it would also mean that whichever family moved into the other's house would thereafter be viewed as inter-lopers.

Mary Anne was particularly relieved to hear the news, since she'd seen the DeWitt-proofing incident first-hand.

As it turned out, not only were Mrs Barrett and Mr DeWitt buying a new house, they were also going to include the seven kids in the house-hunting. And they called the BSC for assistance on the first house-hunting outing.

Shannon and Kristy got the job.

When they got to the Barretts' that Saturday morning, Franklin and his four kids had already arrived in an enormous blue van.

"Cool!" Kristy said to Lindsey, who was sitting in one of the seats by an open window.

Lindsey made a face. Taylor and Madeleine had got out and were playing a half-hearted game of tag in the front garden. Ryan was asleep in his car seat.

Mrs Barrett, holding Marnie, was just coming out of the front door with Suzi and Buddy.

Shannon leaped forward and she and Kristy began to help get seven kids (and two adults) organized for the house-hunting trip.

It wasn't easy. Suzi opened the van door and hopped in, claiming the window seat behind the driver. Taylor immediately said, "That's my seat."

"Huh," said Buddy, rushing to his sister's defence. "Is your name written on it?"

"No, but it's our father's van, so we get first choice."

"Mum, is that true?" wailed Suzi. "I get car sick if I can't look out of the window."

"It's true," said Mrs Barrett, starting to look frazzled already.

"Oooh! Car sick! I'm not sitting next to Suzi," said Taylor, abruptly reversing his position. "She stinks."

"I do not!" shouted Suzi.

"Well, I'm not sitting next to *any* DeWitts. You *all* stink," said Buddy.

"Not like the Barrett Stink Bombs," Lindsey said.

"Enough!" said Kristy, in her best no-nonsense voice.

It silenced both the Barretts and the DeWitts. Soon she and Shannon had all seven kids seated (with Kristy and Shannon in between so that no Barrett was sitting next to a DeWitt and vice versa.)

As they pulled out of the drive, Shannon said, "It's sort of like one of those maths problems in school, you know?"

"Yeah," said Kristy, giving Buddy, who was leaning forward to stick his tongue out at Taylor, a warning look. Buddy leaned back. "Don't ask me how we did it, though!"

She and Shannon thought they were going to have to spend the rest of the house-hunting expedition acting as referees. But halfway through the tour of the first house, they realized they were wrong.

The estate agent kept his smile firmly

in place as the van pulled up at the first house, a split-level ranch house with a fenced-in back garden, and seven kids, two babysitters, and two adults spilled out. "Ah!" he said. "How delightful. What a lovely family you have here."

Shannon and Kristy looked at the agent as if he were nuts, as the DeWitts and the Barretts had taken advantage of the new territory to draw up new lines of battle ("I'm not walking next to her!" "He's got head lice! He touched me, he touched me!")

"I'm sure we have the perfect house for you," the agent went on, leading the way down the wide, straight front path.

Buddy paused to look up and down the pavement. "It's a good pavement for skateboards," he noted. "Smooth. Good kerb."

Lindsey stopped, too, as if struck by what Buddy had said. She studied the pavement for a moment from a couple of angles and then said, "You're right."

It soon became clear that the kids and the adults were looking for somewhat different things in a house.

"Notice the number of built-in cupboards," the agent said, throwing open a door as if he'd built it himself especially for Mr DeWitt and Mrs Barrett.

"Wow, look at that! A tree house!" cried Suzi, running to press her face against the sliding glass door that led from the kitchen to the back porch.

"Great!" cried Taylor, coming to stand next to her. "Look, Madeleine," he said to his sister, whose hand he was holding. "A tree house."

"May we go and look?" Buddy asked Mrs Barrett.

"Of course, of course," said the agent, his big fake smile growing bigger. "It's very sturdy. It's got a safety rail around it."

"A lovely view from the kitchen," said Mr DeWitt as the four kids raced out, followed by Kristy holding Ryan, and Shannon holding Marnie.

"Look at this!" exclaimed Buddy a moment later, leaning on the rail. "You can see *everything*."

While the adults toured the rest of the house, the kids compared notes on the tree house and the back garden.

"Look, it's even got a dog kennel!" cried Lindsey.

"But we haven't got a dog now," said Suzi, looking distressed.

"It can be a guest dog kennel," said Lindsey. "Like a dog hotel."

"And we could use the dog kennel as a fort-in-disguise," said Buddy.

130

"Time to go," said Mr DeWitt.

Everyone piled back in the van, but with a lot fewer complaints and disputes.

"No tree house," said Buddy immediately at the next house.

"Five lovely bedrooms," said the agent, smiling and smiling. "And three baths, including a bath in the master bedroom."

"There are seven of us," said Suzi. "Who gets their own bedroom?"

"Marnie and Ryan can share. They're little. They won't mind," said Buddy.

"Oh! look at this little room," said Suzi. "It's sweet."

"I like this big one," said Taylor. "It's got cool window seats."

"Me, too," said Buddy. He and Taylor looked at each other and so did Shannon and Kristy, waiting for the fight to break out.

Then Buddy said, "We could put a terranium in one of the windows."

Taylor nodded. "Great!" he said.

After that, the kids raced up to each house as if it were a big adventure. While the adults talked about things like dry basements and insulation and solar heating and access to schools, Buddy and Suzi and Taylor and Lindsey and sometimes Madeleine and Marnie and Ryan looked at gardens from a kid's point of view; rated trees for climbing and treehouse potential; timed how long it took to run around the house for future race potential; checked out pavements for skateboard, roller-blade, and bicycle possibilities; and peppered the estate agent with questions about whether they could slide down banisters and how many containers of ice-cream would fit in the freezer in the fridge. They were particularly impressed by one house that had a whole separate freezer in the basement. Buddy estimated that it would hold enough ice-cream for a whole year.

By the time the house-hunting expedition was over, the only point of serious disagreement was over what kind of ice-cream to put in the freezer.

"Maybe we'll get a farm," cried Suzi, her eyes shining, "with horses and goats."

"Horses, horses!" said Marnie, catching her sister's enthusiasm.

"Or a house with a swimming pool," suggested Lindsey.

"Or a farm with a pond," said Buddy.

"For swimming or fishing," Taylor added.

Listening to them talk, Shannon and Kristy were relieved to see that the war between the Barretts and DeWitts was over. From her own experience, Kristy knew that the road ahead would not always be smooth. But the first part, in some ways the hardest part, accepting that things were going to change and looking for the good possibilities in the changes, had begun.

They were on their way to making a new family.

13th CHAPTER

Clover was holding a bowl on her head—right side up. Daffodil was running after her with the hose, trying to fill the bowl up. Both girls were wearing their swimsuits and the sprinkler was on full.

"I'm wet, I'm wet!" shrieked Clover, and I smiled.

I was babysitting for the Austins and I couldn't think of a better place to be on such a hot, hot day.

Still, watching them race through the sprinklers made me tired and thirsty. I decided it was about time they took a break.

"Clover! Daf! Water-break!" I called.

Clover went into peals of laughter and so did Daffodil. "That's funny, Dawn!" shouted Clover.

"No, really, I mean it. Let's have a rest and drink some juice."

"Five more minutes," pleaded Daffodil.

The two stopped and turned to look at me pleadingly.

"I'll get the juice and come back out," I said. "Stay in the garden, OK?"

"OK," said Clover instantly. She took advantage of the moment to dash the contents of her bowl of water on her older sister. Instantly, the two took off through the sprinklers again.

Smiling and shaking my head, I went inside to prepare some orange juice.

Five minutes later I came out on to the back steps. "Drinks. . ." I called. My voice trailed off.

The sprinklers were off. And Clover and Daffodil were nowhere in sight.

I put the tray of juice and glasses down on the table by the steps and checked the garden quickly. Both girls' trainers and T-shirts were missing from the garden chair where they left them.

"Clover! Daffodil!" I called.

No answer. Nevertheless, I checked the front and back gardens thoroughly in case they were hiding, playing a game. But although I looked in every possible place and listened carefully for stifled giggles, I found (and heard) no sign of the two girls.

I didn't panic. Friends had probably

dropped by and the girls, forgetting their promise to stay in the garden, had gone to play with them. But although there were a number of kids up the street, no one had seen Daffodil or Clover.

My heart was beginning to pound heavily now. I had to force myself to stay calm as I went back to the Austins' house and checked it carefully one more time.

No Daffodil. No Clover.

I raced back out of the house and down the pavement towards a group of kids at the other end of the block. They were older boys, unlikely to play with Daf or Clover, but I thought they might have seen something. I was running so fast that I almost knocked over a little boy standing and watching the big boys play basketball.

"Whoa! Sorry," I gasped, grabbing him before he toppled over backwards. "Are you OK?"

He gave me a scornful look, refusing to act like a little kid in front of the big kids. "'Course I am."

On impulse, I said, "You haven't seen two girls go this way? One about your age?" I described what Daffodil and Clover were wearing.

To my surprise—and relief—the little boy nodded.

"Where?" I asked.

He pointed up the pavement. "They were walking with a lady," he said.

"What lady?" I asked. My heart started to hammer. "What did she look like? Tall? Short? Brown hair? Grey hair?"

But he shook his head stubbornly. "A lady. That's all. Just a lady."

Had Daffodil and Clover been kidnapped? I couldn't believe they'd go somewhere with a complete stranger. But I didn't know what else to think, and I couldn't take any chances. And Mrs Austin couldn't be reached straight away. She was at an outdoors craft fair exhibiting her weaving and wouldn't be back till early evening.

I rang the police.

They were there in no time. And before long, a whole group of neighbours, together with my father and Jeff, had spread out to search for Clover and Daffodil.

"I can't believe it," I kept saying. "They were in the back garden. Inside the fence. I just went indoors for a second."

My father patted my shoulder. "Don't worry, Sunshine. They'll turn up. There's probably a perfectly logical explanation for all this."

I wanted to believe him. But I couldn't.

I raced up and down the streets, calling

their names. Then, realizing that I was just covering the same ground that the neighbourhood search party was covering, I left the neighbourhood, still calling, still looking.

But with less and less hope.

Eventually, I found myself looking up at a Ferris wheel. It was the last day of the fair, the one we'd gone to on that disastrous family date with Clarice when I'd got the lime green toy I'd given to Whitney.

Like the whirling in my brain, the Ferris wheel circled and circled. What was I going to do? How was I going to tell Mrs Austin?

Suddenly, my eyes focused. And I couldn't believe what I was seeing. Because going around and around on the Ferris wheel were Daffodil and Clover Austin. Whitney Cater was sitting in the middle with one of the girls on either side.

I was so astonished, I didn't know what to do.

Clover saw me and shouted, "DAWN!" She waved wildly, beaming.

Daffodil smiled, too. Whitney looked at me without any expression at all.

When the Ferris wheel touched down and the girls got off, I rushed up to them. "There you are!" I cried.

"It's so much fun!" cried Clover. "We're going to the funhouse next."

Realizing that they didn't even know they were missing, I took a deep breath. "Maybe in a little while. But right now, we need to get back home. Come on."

"Clover and Daffodil are good," said Whitney, hanging back a little.

"Come on, Whitney," I said. "Help me walk them home."

Whitney nodded and fell into step beside us. I spotted a police officer ahead. "Wait here," I said.

I raced up to the officer and, never taking my eyes off the three as they stood at a little distance, told her what had happened. The officer nodded. "That's what usually happens," she said, getting out her radio to call off the search. "I'm glad that was the case this time, too."

Clover, who had pulled the other two closer, yanked on my arm. "We weren't lost!" she said indignantly. "We were with Whitney!"

"I took care of them," Whitney said. "I was babysitting."

"See?" said Clover.

"What happened?" I asked.

"Whitney came by and asked us to go to the fair while you were inside. She said she was babysitting. We thought it would be OK," said Daffodil.

"But first I made them turn off the sprinklers and put on their shirts and trainers," said Whitney. "That was right."

"Yes, that *was* right," I said. "But you shouldn't have gone anywhere without telling me."

Just then, I looked up and saw a familiar face. "Carol?" I said.

"Dawn! I thought that was you. My girlfriend and I were just buying some candyfloss and I saw you over here. Are you having fun?"

"Ah . . . well," I said.

Carol turned to Whitney and held out her hand. "Hi, I'm Carol."

"How do you do," said Whitney. "I'm Whitney. This is Clover and Daffodil."

"Yes, I'm glad to see you all," said Carol, smiling at them. "You know, Whitney, I watched you earlier on the merry-go-round. You looked like you were having fun."

Carol turned back to me and said, "She was very responsible, making sure the girls didn't get on animals that were too big for them. And she wouldn't let them go on the Zipper."

"See?" said Whitney. "See? I *am*

grown-up! I'm grown-up enough to babysit."

By now, I knew what had happened. Whitney had wanted to prove that she could babysit, too, that she was grown-up. And she *had* done a good job, except that she had taken Clover and Daffodil without telling anyone.

"We've got to go," I said aloud. "It's good to see you again, Carol."

"It's good to see you," Carol told me, and to my surprise, she leaned over and gave me a quick, impulsive hug.

That night, after all the excitement was over, I remembered to tell Dad I'd seen Carol at the fair.

"It was great to see her," I said. "She was terrific. And she was really nice to Whitney."

My father looked pleased. "I'm glad," he said.

"You know," I said slowly, "maybe you should phone her."

I looked down at the toe of my shoe, then up at my father. He wasn't looking at me. He was staring into space, rubbing his chin, a thoughtful smile on his face.

14th CHAPTER

It was time for Whitney and me to have a talk, I decided as I walked over to the Caters' house to begin my last week of babysitting for her. The following Monday, Whitney's day camp programme was going to begin. If she and I didn't settle what had happened between us, we might never get it sorted out at all.

As soon as Mr Cater left for work, I walked over to where Whitney was sitting by the window in the study. She hadn't said hello when I'd come in, but at least she didn't have her back turned to me.

"Whitney, we have to talk," I said.

Whitney looked at me, but she didn't say anything.

"OK. OK, listen. You took really good care of Clover and Daffodil. You were very responsible with them. Everyone says so."

I took a deep breath and Whitney burst out, "See? I can do it! I really can be grown-up! But no one ever listens to me. Especially Mum and Dad."

I didn't smile. I felt a huge twinge of sympathy. We'd all gone through that. We're still going through it, whether it was Stacey's over-protective parents not trusting her enough to be responsible about her diabetes, or Mary Anne's father keeping her in plaits until she was practically grown-up.

Thinking hard, I told Whitney about Mary Anne and about Stacey. And about some of the things that I'd been through, too.

"All of us have had to convince our parents that we're ready for more responsibility. You have to convince your parents, too, Whitney," I concluded.

"I can! I can do things. But they won't let me!"

"You'll have to prove it to them. And I know you can. It might take time, but I know you can."

"How?" asked Whitney.

I paused. We'd all been able to make changes. And although Whitney couldn't make radical changes, some of the things that had worked for us should work for her, too.

"What about this?" I began. "Why don't you make a list of the things you know you can do now, the grown-up things? Not things you can't do, like drive a car, but real things."

Whitney nodded, watching me intently. I went on. "Then show the list to your parents and you decide together which things you can be responsible for now. You can try those things out, and if you do them, then maybe you can add more things to your grown-up list."

"My grown-up list," repeated Whitney. She nodded again and then, for the first time in days, smiled at me. "That's what I'll do, Dawn. Thank you!"

We spent the rest of the afternoon drafting the list. Holding the list in one hand, Whitney walked me to the front door as I was leaving.

I stopped and cleared my throat. "So, Whitney. Good luck with that list."

"Thank you, Dawn," said Whitney.

"There's something else. Do you think we could be friends now, as well as, well, babysitter and babysittee?"

Whitney frowned, then smiled again. "We can be both," she agreed.

"I'm glad," I said.

144

"Me, too," said Whitney. "Me, too."

A couple of days later, the We ♥ Kids Club met and I made a proposal: that Whitney be made an honorary club member and maybe special helper, to accompany us on some jobs, like babysitting for Clover and Daffodil Austin. I didn't have to convince Sunny that Whitney was great with kids.

"You should see her," she told the club. "She's great. She really plays with the kids and she's great at thinking up games. She's very, very careful too. Clover and Daffodil *loved* her."

Not that we needed much convincing. But Sunny's words made me feel good inside. I coughed to get everyone's attention, then called for a vote.

Unanimous. It was official. Whitney Cater was now an Honorary Member and Special Helper in the We ♥ Kids Club.

I could hardly wait to let Whitney know. I decided to tell her on the last day I sat for her.

"Let's go and sit on the swings in the back garden," I suggested.

"OK," said Whitney.

We swung to and fro for a little while. But I could tell Whitney's heart wasn't in it. After a minute or two, she stopped.

"I'm going to miss you, Dawn."

"I'll miss you, too. Whitney. But I've got some good news. So maybe you won't miss me too much."

"I will miss you," insisted Whitney.

"Not if you are an Honorary Member and Special Helper in the We Love Kids Club," I said. "Which you officially are. We voted you in on Wednesday. That means you'll be helping us out on special babysitting jobs."

Whitney's mouth opened and then closed. "A member?" she managed to say at last. "Of your club? I'm a babysitter!"

"Yes!"

With a whoop, Whitney pumped her swing high in the air, then jumped off, her eyes sparkling.

"Me?" she kept saying. "Me? In your club?"

"That's the deal," I said. "What do you think?"

"Yes!" shouted Whitney. Then she made herself serious for a moment. "Yes, thank you, Dawn. I'd like that."

But the seriousness couldn't last and a moment later she was dancing around me, laughing with delight.

It was a great afternoon. I didn't want it to end. But I knew now there would be other, different afternoons to which I could look forward with Whitney.

146

And as I was leaving, after giving Whitney a big bear hug and getting one back, I knew that Whitney and I would remain friends.

I reached up and touched the friendship necklace. Whitney had given it back to me. Friends again.

Friends for ever.

15th CHAPTER

With the end of my job with Whitney, life got a little less hectic. I relaxed and devoted some time to the beach, working on my surfing and giving my full support to the perfect days that kept arriving one after the other.

Whitney was doing well in her new day camp. And one Saturday, she and Sunny and Clover and Daffodil and I went on a special babysitters excursion to the park. Needless to say, it was a big success—as good as the best surfboard ride.

Another part of life slowed down a bit, too. Dad stopped dating so much. He turned up for dinner more often, and even cooked a few weird Dad meals, like tofu-turkey casserole.

Surprise. Some things aren't meant to be eaten, even if they're good for you! We ended up going out for pizza and having a great time.

I wondered if that last date with Alana-the-Pain and Kayla had put Dad off dating for ever. I wasn't sure how I felt about that. I liked having him around. But from time to time, I thought I saw a sort of lonely look on his face.

Then things picked up a bit and I knew he'd started dating again. He didn't mention her name, but Jeff and I braced ourselves for another family outing.

"Maybe it'll be to the zoo," said Jeff one night, "and we can feed her to the bears."

"Poor bears," I said, thinking back over some of the family date disasters.

We didn't ask Dad what was happening. We decided, by mutual unspoken agreement, that it was better not to know.

Then one day, Dad said casually, as he was putting on his jacket, "So, I'll be going out with someone you know tonight, you two."

Jeff clutched his throat and fell over backwards. "Kayla!"

Dad smiled and shook his head.

"*Not* Karina!" I gasped.

Rolling his eyes, Dad shook his head again. "I'll put you all out of your misery. It's Carol."

"Carol! Wow!" said Jeff.

"Cool," I said. I suddenly suspected that it had been Carol he'd been seeing all along.

But Dad didn't say anything more about her after his date and he didn't mention any family dates.

Finally, one night after dinner was over, Dad began to gather up the plates. "I'll just get this into the kitchen and then we'll have dessert," he said.

"Jeff and I can get that," I said.

"Thanks," said Jeff.

"No, no," Dad insisted. "I'll get it."

He rushed to and fro, clearing the table and bringing out all the dessert things. Except the ice-cream. Instead he sat down at the table and stared at us.

"Dad?" I prompted.

"Where's the ice-cream?" asked Jeff.

"How would you feel about having Carol as your stepmother?" Dad burst out. "I know we've been through this before, and I. . ."

"Carol?" said Jeff. "Carol's OK." He frowned. "Can I go and get the ice-cream?"

"Go and get the ice-cream, Jeff," I said. Good grief! Dad dishes out some major news and all Jeff can think about is ice-cream.

150

As Jeff disappeared in the direction of the kitchen I looked at my dad. He was smiling. He looked relaxed and happy and pleased with himself.

And suddenly I was happy and pleased, too. "I think it would be great, Dad. You and Carol."

Maybe that's what all those weird dates had been about, after all. Maybe Dad had been thinking about Carol and that's why he'd gone out with such strange people— people who couldn't possibly replace Carol.

I remembered Carol shaking hands with Whitney and smiled even more. "Great," I said again.

Jeff reappeared with ice-cream and a bigger spoon for himself and we concentrated on dessert after that—on dessert and a special dinner Dad wanted to have for Carol to celebrate and "make everything official".

We spent one day planning the menu and two days getting the dinner ready, including old-fashioned bread rolls that had to rise *three* times, a special pasta sauce that had to sit for twenty-four hours, and three kinds of appetizers.

Carol's eyes widened when she saw the table (which we'd set up outside) with the candles and tablecloth and fresh flowers on it. "It's lovely," she said.

"For our special guest," I said, bowing a little.

Jeff snorted, but you could tell he was excited, too.

The meal went perfectly. Jeff and I kept exchanging pleased glances, but Dad just kept looking at Carol. She kept looking at him, too, and maybe she didn't taste anything we'd cooked after all, but she did remember to say, from time to time, "This is wonderful," and "I love this. It's delicious."

When the meal was over and we'd brought out dessert and coffee (and more milk for Jeff and raspberry juice for me), Dad cleared his throat.

"As you know, this is a very special occasion. We have a special guest here. She's been here before, so I don't need to introduce her."

"Is it Carol?" my brother the wit asked.

"Give the boy in the striped shirt the prize," I said. "Be quiet, Jeff."

Grinning, Jeff rolled his eyes at me. Carol saw him and smiled.

Dad went on. "But we don't want to think of Carol as a special guest any more."

Dad stopped and suddenly sounded a lot less formal. And a lot more nervous.

"So," he said.

"Go on, Dad. You can do it," urged Jeff.

"Jeff!" I said.

"Just say it!" Jeff jumped out of his chair, threw himself on one knee, and spread his arms out. "Carol, will you marry me?" he said, and clasped his hands over his heart and fell over backwards.

Carol laughed and leaned forward to help Jeff up. Then she stopped and gasped. She turned to my Dad and her face went bright pink.

"Is Jeff. . ." She began and stopped. She tried again. "Did you. . ." She stopped once more.

"Dad!" I said.

Dad's face was as pink as Carol's. "If you say yes," he said, "you'll be saying yes to me. And to these two here, too. I . . . wanted us to be in this together."

"Oh!" Carol threw her arms around our father and hugged him so hard he almost fell over to join Jeff.

"It's about time," Jeff complained.

After that (while Jeff concentrated as usual on dessert), we made wedding plans. By the time Dad got up to walk Carol to her car and say goodnight, we knew the wedding was going to be in December, that I was going to be the maid of honour, and that Jeff was going to be the best man.

I could hardly wait.

I went to bed that night on a cloud of excitement. But I didn't go to sleep straight away. I had one more thing to do to make it a perfect end to a perfect day.

I picked up the phone and punched in the number.

"Hello?" I said. "Mary Anne? It's me. Guess what? You're going to love this. There's going to be another wedding in the family!"